Between the Shady Groves

RASPBERRY RIDGE
BOOK TEN

JESSIE GUSSMAN

Acknowledgments

Cover art by Julia Gussman
Editing by Heather Hayden
Narration by Jay Dyess
Author Services by CE Author Assistant

Listen to the unabridged audio for FREE performed by Jay Dyess on the Say with Jay channel on YouTube. Get early access to all of Jay's recordings and listen to Jessie's books before they're available to the general public, plus get daily Bible readings by Jay and bonus scenes by becoming a Say with Jay channel member.

One

Lauren Knodel pushed the key into the old-fashioned lock and wiggled it gently. There was a knack to this old thing, and she finally felt it click. Then, she turned it, and the lock sprung.

She braced herself, taking a deep breath and closing her eyes for a moment, before she pushed open the door to her mother's bakery—empty and abandoned on the main street of Raspberry Ridge—and stepped inside.

It had been years since she'd been in here, but everything looked the same. Her mother always left those big bowls on the back shelf. Her mixer was spotlessly clean. It was her pride and joy. An expensive piece of equipment that she had saved for years to buy when Lauren had been younger. Lauren remembered the celebration when her mom had finally been able to purchase it and how she had guarded it fiercely, protecting it and yet showing it off by making everything visible from the other side of the counter.

In fact, almost everything that her mom did in the bakery was visible from the other side of the counter. It was one of the reasons why folks in Raspberry Ridge had always loved her shop. It wasn't just a bakeshop with amazing smells and tantalizing desserts. It was a place where one could go to learn, be entertained, see what was on the menu, and actually see it be prepared. There were no secrets.

Even now, a yeasty smell rose around her, mixed in with the dust. A little bit of vanilla, cinnamon, and Lauren could close her eyes and see her mother pulling a tray of puffy golden cinnamon buns out of one of the double ovens built into the wall.

She would have the icing ready and smooth it on while the buns were still hot. There would be a line of people waiting to purchase them, and the cinnamon buns would be gone before the pan cooled.

Her mother had a touch, a gift, and her mom had always said that Lauren had inherited it. Lauren hadn't wanted to have anything to do with it.

She sighed, closing her eyes and stepping in, closing the door behind her before opening her eyes again and looking around trying to figure out what had changed.

Her. She had changed. She had grown from the spoiled, immature, egotistical girl who thought she knew everything but really knew nothing.

Deep inside, she had been scared and intimidated and petrified, and the tragedy that she had been a part of had attached to her, chasing her from this small lakeside community to the city of Cincinnati, where she worked for a while before she fell in love and got married.

And then, after three miscarriages, a lot of miscommunication, and the death of her mom—she decided to pack up and come back.

She spent years caring for her mother. All for naught.

Now, she needed to figure out what to do with this, her mother's pride and joy. The shop where her mom had lovingly prepared each and every delectable dessert and baked good that she'd happily sold to her friends and neighbors. She fed her daughter here, made a living here, and they lived in the back and upstairs. There was a bit of a backyard with a shady grove of peach trees providing shade in the summer, delicious fruit in the fall, and the promise of both of those things all winter long, as the bare branches reached to the sky.

Even now, the tiny fruits were growing, ripening, getting ready to burst into flavor and juicy deliciousness in another month or two.

The trees had been neglected for years, and Lauren had no idea whether they would bear good fruit in their neglected state or not.

Her mom had always cultivated them, pruned them, and sometimes even sprayed them. But Lauren had done nothing. She had been too busy caring for her mom and ignoring her failing marriage while it fell apart.

Her jaw tightened, and she stopped thinking about peach trees so that she could stop thinking about her marriage. It was as dead as the branches in winter.

Even if she didn't have an official divorce yet. Cannon, her husband, would soon file. He wasn't the kind of man who would be alone for long. Successful and charismatic, good at his job, building a million-dollar business from nothing, he would be a catch for someone. Lauren turned away, her eyes sweeping the storefront once again.

She didn't know what to do. She couldn't go back. And she didn't know how to move forward. Unless she opened her mother's shop again. But...could she?

She didn't know how to run a business, had never paid attention. Her husband had done it, her mama had done it before that. But her? She worked at a job, but she knew that running a business was different. There was so much more responsibility. A person didn't just work the job, they had to do pricing and inventory and taxes and all the backend things, like making sure that there was insurance, and what about employees?

She had no idea how to do any of it.

Not for the first time, she wished for Cannon's wise advice. He was a good man. A really good man. But...the years of taking care of her mom and the miscarriages that she'd endured before that had taken their toll on their marriage, and their communication had become almost nonexistent. They allowed their relationship to die. And she walked away.

Is that what happened? she questioned herself, because she wasn't sure anymore. Losing her mom had taken the last of her strength, the last of her will to explore and challenge and thrive. She just wanted to curl into a ball and do nothing. What was this? Depression? This weight on her chest, this dark cloud hanging over her, and the idea that life would never be fun again.

Maybe it was the idea that she had missed so much of her mom's life because she'd been selfish. She pursued what she wanted and hadn't considered how devastated her mom must have felt to have her only daughter leave, and not just leave, but leave with a big smile on her face and an attitude of "this town isn't good enough for me, I need to find something big enough to hold me."

She had basically thumbed her nose at everything her mama built, the town that she moved to to raise her, and the friends and neighbors who had supported her throughout her childhood.

She walked over to the place where the counter folded up. She lifted up the moveable piece, like she had a million times in childhood, and slipped through so she stood behind the counter, where her mom practically lived.

She took a few more steps to her mother's prized mixer, the huge one that sat on the low shelf built just for it and could hold enough dough to feed the town.

It was the one that her mom had used every morning after that glorious day when she had finally been able to afford to buy it.

Lauren tested it with her fingers, sliding them over it, seeing the dust rub off the mixer, and thinking about her mom and the many hours that this mixer had spent turned on in the kitchen, with townspeople laughing and joking at the few tables that were set around, or sitting at the bar, while her mom made them their specialty coffees, getting more and more complicated over the years, and shared laughter and tears and life together.

Her mom had known just how to do all of that. To handle it all so perfectly. To balance the intricacies of making a business profitable, making a living from it, and still having friendships and feelings and making people feel like her shop was their second home.

But now, her mom was gone. All the wisdom, all the recipes, all the knowledge. It was all just memories. Whatever was left.

She took a breath, and her stomach growled. She realized she hadn't eaten since the day before, sometime. Maybe breakfast? She wasn't sure. She had driven here from Cincinnati and slept upstairs. The apartment held memories too, but not like this did. This was where life happened.

She had bought a few groceries at the store in Blueberry Beach, the last one she passed before she got here. Enough groceries to make her mom's specialty. Nutella banana bread. It was easy but so, so good. It had been her favorite back in high school. She didn't know when Nutella came out, but her mom had discovered it at some point, and it instantly skyrocketed to Lauren's favorite baked good of all time. She had gotten the recipe from her mom, and it had become her signature bread. That, along with the cheesy bread that her mom made so well—she had a knack for it too, and most people said she made it even better than her mom.

That would take a little while, but on a whim, she had brought the ingredients for that as well.

First, she needed to clean the dust off the equipment and the counters and...wade through the memories so that she could possibly pick up the pieces of her life.

She thought about her husband, the life she had expected to build with him. It was her fault as much as his. She had to take the blame where it was due. She had been devastated by the miscarriages, and...it seemed like he didn't care. And then, with her mom getting sick, she moved her mom in and put all of her being into caring for her mom. There hadn't been anything left for her husband. That had been on her.

But her husband had been busy working, making his business successful, and basically paying for everything. She had quit her job as a teacher so that she could stay home and be with her mom. She hadn't even talked to her husband about it; she had just done it.

He'd not complained. He was a good man. Still, it was hard to forgive him for the fact that he couldn't comfort her in her loss. Not over their children, not over her mom. He just kept working.

It irritated her to the point she couldn't stand it anymore.

Plus, she had a deep longing to come home. And now, she was finally here. All she had to do was figure out how she was going to make a living. If she could open the baked goods shop and make it as successful as her mom had over the years. Or was the era of the small mom-and-pop bakery completely over?

Two

C annon Knodel flipped his phone back and forth in his hand. End over end.

Lauren had left a short note, packed a few things, and left.

End over end.

He held the note in his other hand. It didn't say much. He supposed that nothing it said was surprising, either. He just...felt surprised anyway.

He pressed his lips together and continued to flip the phone while pacing to the window and then going back.

She left yesterday. Which was interesting timing on her part, since she knew he would be gone overnight for a job in Chicago. He never turned down the Chicago jobs. They were more lucrative than anything else he had.

Being in Cincinnati, it was quite a drive, but he had more than one job. His reputation had spread, and he had jobs in Pittsburgh, Cleveland, and even down to Lexington, Kentucky.

But the Chicago jobs were the cream of the crop.

Most of the time, he sent a crew out, and it took them a couple of days. But as the owner of the business, he always showed up.

The paper crinkled in his hand, and he looked at it once more.

Dear Cannon,

I suppose it will be a relief to you to know that I'm moving out. Now that Mom's gone, the apartment is empty without her and even emptier when you're not around. I know you know I hoped to have children, and that doesn't seem to be in the cards for us. Anyway, that's not your fault.

You can do what you need to do. It's fine. I understand. Let me know how you want to proceed.

I wish things could have been different.

Lauren

Cannon pursed his lips and gripped the paper tight, causing it to crinkle in his hands, as he walked back to the window, looking out at the back of the neighbor's house. It wasn't much of a view.

They could have upgraded. He was making good money now, and even without Lauren's salary, they could have afforded a much nicer place. Instead, the nest egg in their checking account had been growing bigger and bigger. He needed to take some time to figure out investments, but he hadn't done that because his business had been so busy. And so profitable.

Now, it looked like...it didn't matter?

He wasn't quite sure why she had left him a paper message. She had his phone number. It wasn't like she couldn't have texted him. Even if she decided that she wanted to talk. Or that she wanted to meet somewhere, or that she just wanted to go out on a date. When was the last time they'd gone out on a date?

Before her mother had come to stay. When she moved in, both of them knew that it was most likely going to end with the death of her mom. Even though it had taken years. The doctors hadn't had much hope from the beginning, and chemo had been harsh and long. Her mom had rallied, beating back the disease to begin with, and Lauren's hopes had lifted. His had too. Her mom was impossible not to love. Kind and effusive, friendly and energetic, she was like a carbon copy of her daughter, Lauren.

He'd fallen in love with Lauren, head over heels, the first time they met, when he had gone to put a security system in her neighbor's home. She'd been out tending a couple of saplings she'd planted in her backyard. Her postage stamp-sized backyard. He had wondered why she even bothered. With all the houses around, it was unlikely the trees were going to get any sunlight or thrive at all.

Still, she'd been happy and smiling and sweet, and he'd known that he didn't want to live his life without her from that very first meeting.

But now, now it appeared that he was going to be living life without her anyway. But why? What had he done wrong? What had changed? Sure, they weren't really talking, but she'd been busy with her mom, he'd been busy with his job, his business, trying to make sure all the bills were paid and...riding the wave of prosperity. He figured that it probably wouldn't last long, and he wanted to take advantage of it while he could. He was doing it for them. Didn't she know that?

He took a breath and then walked back to the middle of the kitchen floor. It wasn't far. The kitchen was small, as was the apartment. Two bedrooms. One for his wife and him, one for her mother. She had taken to sleeping in her mother's room on a small cot once her mother had gotten bad sometime last year. Maybe it was the year before. He didn't know.

There was a part of him that had been a little relieved when the third pregnancy had ended in miscarriage. Not that he was happy, just that he knew that they would have had to move, in amongst her mom's treatments and his job and her caretaking. After all, they didn't have any family nearby to help.

It made sense to him, but Lauren had been devastated. And he understood. Or at least thought he did. He wasn't happy that they had lost a child, but he didn't see it as the end of the world. Sure, it was her third miscarriage, but...eventually things would work out. Surely. And maybe God was just doing this so that they could have better accommodations when they actually did have a child.

Was he being uncaring or unfeeling?

A couple of guys at work had laughed when he had mentioned it, and had said something about their wives not allowing them to think that way or something.

He hadn't really paid attention. Lauren was the perfect wife. And he loved her with everything he had.

And now she was gone.

He sank slowly into a chair, still holding the paper. What was he going to do?

Three

The familiar hum of the little counter mixer filled the small bakery.

Lauren had spent the last several hours cleaning off the counters, wiping them down. She had tested the large mixer and taken the bowl off to clean it, but she wasn't using it now. She wasn't making enough banana bread to feed the entire town. She was just making something for herself. To help heal her heart. It seemed like her mom always had some kind of special baked good for whatever hurt and pain she had.

"Hello," a voice said as the bell above the door jingled. That was another familiar sound.

Lauren spun around, her hand going to her chest.

If Cannon were there, he would castigate her for not making sure the door was locked. After all, he specialized in security and had heard his share of stories about break-ins and robberies and even rapes and murders because people weren't properly protected. A lot of times, his company was called after just such a tragedy, and Cannon would shake his head and say, "Too little, too late."

Those were some of his biggest customers though, since people who had just experienced a tragedy like that were determined that they weren't going to experience another one.

"Hello. I'm sorry, I should have locked the door. I'm not open."

"Lauren?" the woman said, and Lauren looked a little closer. Did she know this person? She supposed she did look familiar.

"I'm Grace Honea. Well, Grace Gillett now."

"Grace. Oh my goodness." Lauren looked harder at the woman who stood in front of her. Yes, she could see her high school friend Grace in there. The woman was older with a few lines around her face and mouth, her skin still glowing, but not with youth. More with vitality. And honey blonde hair—a dead ringer for her memories of the friend from her high school and childhood.

"Wow. I didn't think I'd recognize you, but now that you've said who you are, you haven't changed much at all."

"Neither have you. Older, like all of us, but still just as beautiful and with a smile that lights up the room." Grace came over, lifting the countertop easily and slipping through like it had been just yesterday the last time she'd done it. Grace, Lauren, Claire, and Yolanda had been inseparable ever since she could remember.

Until Yolanda wasn't with them anymore.

Lauren blinked just a bit, pushing that thought away. That wasn't something she thought about, because the guilt and pain of her role in all of that was all-consuming. She couldn't stand how she felt, the guilt and how she knew that it was all her fault.

She switched the mixer off and then turned around, surprised when Grace had her arms around her and was pulling her into a huge hug.

"It's been so long," she said, hugging Grace back and trying to pretend that it wasn't uncomfortable for her.

She supposed she had kind of gotten out of the habit of touching people. Where they lived in Cincinnati, it wasn't in the heart of the city, definitely not downtown, but she had close neighbors, and they were city neighbors. Not the small-town kind, who hugged without reserve and talked about everything.

She wasn't even sure what the neighbors on the left or right of them were named. And she didn't even know quite how many people lived in the house across the street.

She supposed those people knew her just as well and probably didn't even notice that she'd left.

"I heard about your mom," Grace said as she pulled back.

"Yeah. That was hard."

Grace nodded. "I kept hoping she'd get better and come back. We all miss her."

"You live here now?" Lauren said. She was almost positive that Grace and Claire had both moved away around the time she had. They might have been back for summers in college, but according to her mom, she hadn't seen them much at all.

"Yeah. Not that long ago. Claire's back too."

Lauren nodded. Not really wanting to get the gang together again. There were too many memories, and they weren't easy ones. Although, there were a lot of good ones.

It's just the good ones were overshadowed by all of the bad.

"That's nice. I... I'm not sure I'm back to stay. I needed to do something with this." She didn't want to get into everything. About her mom dying, and her not being happy in her marriage, and drifting apart from her husband and leaving him. He hadn't done anything wrong, and she was a little embarrassed to admit that she just walked out. It would be hard to explain to someone who didn't understand that they just didn't talk anymore. It was like living with a stranger. It had to be that way for him too, and she didn't want to hold him back. He deserved a good woman. He was a good man.

And she felt like a shell of herself.

Not to mention the black cloud that hung over her, hot and heavy.

"Well, whether you stay or whether you don't, I'd love to get together with you sometime. I...don't want to barge in if you're dealing with memories." She looked around. "It feels like yesterday that your mom was standing behind the counter laughing and making her cinnamon rolls and the most delicious coffee anyone ever made anywhere. I think she always put extra caramel in mine, because I can't get anything else to taste as good."

"Yeah. Mom just had a knack for those kinds of things."

"You're like a carbon copy of your mom. You have a knack for those things too." Grace narrowed her eyes and looked at her like she was looking over a pair of wire-rimmed glasses like a schoolmarm.

Lauren had a look like that. She'd used it in the classroom often enough. But she didn't like it being used on her. Not by her friend, and not when she said something like that. Like Lauren should be able to easily pick up where her mom left off and carry on. It felt like the shoes that she was trying to put on were sixteen sizes too big, and she would never be able to fit into them.

"I don't really have a knack for anything." She didn't even have a knack for caretaking. After all, her mama had died.

"Is everything okay?" Grace asked with far too much perception. Lauren just wanted to be left alone. To curl up and hide. Except, she wanted to be here in the bakery too. Because it was here in the bakery where she felt the closest to her mom.

"Everything's just fine," she lied through her teeth. "I just wanted some time alone to process. You know. Sometimes you need to do that when you have big changes in your life."

To say the least. Change was the right word though. Not only was her mom dead, but so was her marriage. However, she wasn't going to go into that with Grace.

"Would you at least try to be able to spend some time with me before you have to leave?" Grace asked, sounding so humble and hopeful that Lauren couldn't tell her no.

"Sure. Say when." It wasn't like she had a job or anything.

"Tomorrow. In the afternoon. We could meet at the healing garden. Have you seen it?"

"No. I just got in last night and didn't do anything more than step out back and look at the peach trees."

"They're so beautiful. Your backyard was one of my favorite spots in town growing up. Besides here. But you'll love the healing garden. There are shady groves there too. And a path that walks between them. It's...beautiful and calming and healing too."

It was like Grace somehow knew that something inside of her needed to be healed. Although, Lauren highly doubted a garden would be able to do that.

"Sure. We'll meet between the shady groves. What time?" she asked, wondering if she could possibly have something come up that would make it so that she couldn't make it.

"Would two o'clock work?" Grace asked, and she nodded.

It wasn't like she had anything planned. "Two o'clock should be fine."

"Could I ask—would you mind if Claire came too? If she's able to. She's moved back permanently as well, and you would not believe who she's with."

"No, I probably wouldn't," she said, not wanting to hear it, but Grace either didn't hear that tone in her voice or ignored it.

"She's with Josiah McMurtry, and would you believe that Trevor and I are together? We just got married a couple weeks ago, and it was almost like Claire decided that they were going to beat us, because they got married a few days before we did." She laughed, like it was somehow funny.

"Well, good for you," Lauren said and watched as Grace's face fell as though she was hurt by her lack of interest and enthusiasm.

Unfortunately, Lauren just couldn't drum up anything else. It was like her emotions were dead, along with her mom and her marriage.

"All right. I'll leave you. I really am looking forward to getting together with you. And I know that Claire will be excited when I tell her that you're in town. We talked about how much we miss you."

"Okay. I'll see you tomorrow. Between the shady groves."

She didn't want to go to the healing garden. She didn't want to meet her friends, she didn't want to do anything, other than just sit here and wallow in the memories and bathe in her sadness and depression and all the terrible things she wished she could change.

Grace was barely out of the door when Lauren turned the mixer back on, after scraping down the sides of the bowl.

She had mixed it long enough. She probably mixed it too long. It was going to be tough and not light and airy like it should be. But she didn't care. It was the smell she wanted, more than the food. She probably wouldn't even eat it. Her appetite had been fickle lately and more gone than come.

Stopping the mixer, she scraped the bowl again and then poured the batter into the pans that she had already greased and prepared. The oven had been preheated, because she had been trained by the best, and she plopped the pans in, eager to have the scent of the Nutella bread spilling through the bakery again.

While she waited for it to bake, she did what her mom had always taught her to do. Cleaned up immediately. She could almost hear her mom say that it was easier to clean up a small mess than a big one. So she liked to keep her space wiped clean and her dishes done.

She had taught Lauren to do the same.

Lauren wasn't sure she had learned a whole lot from her mom. It seemed like there was so much she didn't know and more she wished she would have paid attention to, but that was one of the things she was sure about. If one made a mess, one cleaned it up immediately, because a fresh mess was easier to clean up than an old mess, and a small one easier than a large one.

Maybe that's what she had done—she had waited too long to clean up the mess of her marriage, and it was just too big for her to be able to do anything with.

Cannon, I wish you were here. I miss you.

Four

"All right. I want you to keep me abreast of everything. You can text me, and I'll help you as much as I can. But I need to have the next six weeks off and be interrupted as little as possible."

"All right," George said, looking at the iPad screen that showed the schedule for the next six weeks. George had been a dependable foreman for years, and now, Cannon was going to completely depend on him.

"Do you have any questions?" Cannon asked, wishing he'd given George more responsibilities over the years. But he was the kind of business owner who liked to be hands-on and doing everything himself. He never guessed that he would need to take this kind of time off. But he knew it was absolutely essential. In fact, it might be too late. And then... He wasn't sure what he was going to do.

Even if it wasn't too late, he wasn't sure what he was going to do, because it was obvious that his wife was...not happy. To say the least.

She hadn't answered any of his texts, hadn't even responded, and he wondered if maybe she'd changed her number or blocked his. He didn't know how to tell.

"No. I don't. I'm sure it might be a little bit rocky, but I'll deal with it. I know how to put these things together, and Remy in the office can take care of the billing and all that."

"Yeah. The girls in the office have things covered. If you've got the outside stuff covered, they've got the inside stuff covered, and Micah and Shelley will hopefully keep the sales rolling in." That was the one place where he really didn't spend a whole lot of time. Word-of-mouth was their sales for them, but they had Micah and Shelley who went to trade shows and worked on marketing. It had been more than enough to keep them busier than they could handle.

Maybe Lauren was upset about her mom passing away. Or something else. Maybe he needed to find her and spend a little time holding her hand. But he was almost sure she would come out of it. Lauren was happy and upbeat, and whatever the issue was, they would work it out.

There was one small problem.

He didn't know where she was.

"All right. I will only be gone as long as I need to be to get some personal things straightened up. Then I'll be back."

He didn't really think it was that serious. Six weeks might be too much. Still, he'd never left his business for that long, and he was a little nervous about leaving it now. But his wife and marriage meant a lot to him, and he wasn't going to just let her go. He wanted to fix this. Any rational man would, of course. There was no cheating happening, unless there was something he didn't know. And if there was, they were going to have to talk. If she was cheating on him...

The thought made his heart race, and despite himself, his pace picked up. He headed to his truck, and he was going to go to her sister-in-law's house first. A call might make more sense, but he felt the need to move. If she wasn't there, in Lexington, Kentucky, then he was going to look in Raspberry Ridge. Her mom still had a place there, and it had been left to Lauren in her mom's will. They had talked about using it as a summer house, but he had been reluctant to do that, since he didn't want to leave his business for the summer. Or even for a couple of weeks.

In hindsight, maybe he should have been more open to the idea. It probably meant something to her.

Still, they could work it out. He got in his truck and pointed it south.

$$Five$$

"Knock, knock," a male voice said, lifting Lauren out of her deep thoughts as she sat at a table, her untouched Nutella banana bread in front of her. The scent had been all she needed. It smelled like her mom and home and safety and love and comfort and everything she didn't have in her marriage or her life right now. She just wanted to sit at the table, lost in her memories, soaking in the scent.

But her head turned toward the door. This wasn't someone she recognized at all.

It was a man, about her age, maybe slightly older, but still mid-thirties. He had a short, military-type haircut and a couple of days' growth of beard on his face, but it didn't hide the square jaw that jutted out under intelligent, inquisitive, and aware blue eyes. Those eyes scanned the bakery as though he were scoping out a sniper nest in Afghanistan or some other war-torn country. He walked with that smooth, catlike grace that reminded her of military too.

His clothes didn't really say much, other than casual, with worn blue jeans that looked like they were older than she was and a T-shirt that fit snugly around a chest that spent a lot of time in the weight room.

She blinked. She hadn't realized there were actual men like this walking the streets. She thought they were only found in romance novels.

"Hello?" she said, and then she shook her head. "I'm not actually open. I'm sorry if the smell drew you in."

"It did. You must be piping scent into the outdoors or something, because I was taking my daily walk to the beach, and...I kind of felt a little bit like the children following the Pied Piper. There wasn't anything I could do but turn in here."

He was charming too. With a dimple she could see through the scruff when he smiled. Straight white teeth. An easygoing way about him, despite the awareness in his eyes.

This was a man she should feel safe with.

Of course, she felt safe with her husband too. He just...wasn't that interested in her.

"I'm sorry. I guess the least I can do is offer you a loaf to take with you." She stood, knowing she had one entire loaf that she hadn't cut, and she definitely wasn't going to eat it before it spoiled. She hadn't even taken a bite of the first one. Although she could tell that it would taste really good. She had cooked it to perfection, just like her mom and just like she expected of herself.

"You aren't going to have to twist my arm in order to get me to take it. But I'm opening a bookstore next door, and in return, I can offer you one free book. You look like...a thriller reader."

She laughed. "Good guess. Considering that thrillers are the number one seller in America. But no. I'm more romance, or maybe women's fiction." She had never been able to get into thrillers. They were too scary, and after reading them, she couldn't sleep. She couldn't understand how others could read that kind of stuff and still live with themselves.

"Romance was my next guess. Mostly because it's the number two genre in the US. You're right. I was playing averages."

She nodded. "I figured."

She had gone behind the counter, leaving it open, but he didn't follow her. She didn't really expect him to. Customers never did. It was just the people who were familiar, close, friends.

"Give me a second, I'll wrap this up for you." She used a knife to gently cut around the banana bread pan, loosening it from the sides, and then she turned it upside down on top of the freshly cleaned counter.

It came out perfectly. Then she grabbed some plastic wrap from the drawer. It was right where it was supposed to be, like it had been just yesterday that her mom had closed the shop and gone with her back to Cincinnati.

She remembered that day like it was yesterday, but it had been almost five years ago.

"Boy, after this I might owe you two books."

"You don't really look like a bookseller to me," she said casually, wondering what a guy like that was doing opening a bookstore.

"My uncle owned the gaming store. I don't know if you grew up in this town, but you might remember it."

"Yeah. It was video games, TVs, and radios. I remember it well." It was a little outdated even when she had been young, but Butch Connolly, the guy who owned it, had made it work.

"Yeah. I guess it was an electronics store or something. I wasn't here much. But he left it to me in his will."

"And you're not an electronics guy? Somehow I have trouble believing that." She looked him over again. He definitely looked like he knew how to wiretap telephones and use all kinds of specialized communication hardware.

"I used to be. But gaming is addictive to me, and I better not own a store with games in it. I would end up spending all my time playing and not selling. Books are safer." He winked at her.

Was he flirting? She wasn't quite sure. She was in her mid-thirties and hadn't thought about flirting for more than a decade. She ignored it. It was better to assume he wasn't. Maybe he had something in his eye.

"I guess it's kind of like me opening a baked goods store. I am afraid I might eat my profits and come down with some dread disease—heart disease, diabetes, cancer. Something from all the stuff I make." She supposed that's what happened to her mom. Although her mom had never been extra heavy. She had just been...pleasantly plump. That's how Lauren looked at her anyway. She supposed that in today's medical models, her mom would have been obese. She was sliding toward that herself.

Maybe that's why Cannon never paid much attention to her. She was less appealing to him than she was when she was younger and thinner.

"I hope that doesn't change your mind. I wouldn't mind having a baked goods store right next door to me. Plus, you could sell healthy stuff too."

"Like smoothies and yogurt parfaits?" She smiled. The store just wouldn't be the same. But she supposed she could sell them on the side. That would be the downside of having a baked goods store. She wouldn't really be helping people, although... Was there something to be said for food that warmed the stomach and the heart? Even if it wasn't good for the heart?

She had to think on that. Maybe it was more of a moral issue than she realized. Maybe she should just go back to her husband. And leave this town, these memories, and this intriguing man behind.

She finished wrapping up the banana bread, and walking back, she stayed on her side of the counter, handing it over. For some reason, she thought it might be a good idea to keep some distance between her and this man. Not that she was exceptionally attracted or even interested in him. He just seemed like a dangerous type. Plus, she might have left her husband, but she was still good and solidly married. She was thankful she hadn't left her wedding rings behind. She assumed that Cannon would file for divorce, and she would go along with it. But she wasn't taking her rings off until it was time.

"Thanks. That was awfully kind of you. I promise I won't come over looking for handouts all the time."

The man was charming, but he didn't seem like much of a people person either. "You don't need to promise. I'm not worried about it. I... haven't decided whether I'm going to open the shop or not." She paused for a moment, and then she said, "My mom used to own it. There are a lot of memories here for me."

He nodded, acknowledging her words. "I guess that'll be a hard decision."

He didn't seem overly interested in what she had to say. She supposed that was a typical man. Focused on whatever had their attention and whatever they were trying to accomplish. Anything else was just noise.

She didn't mean to lump all men into that category, but maybe she was expecting too much of her husband. Maybe men didn't sit around with their arms around their wives comforting them when they needed it. Maybe that was just something from a romance novel. Maybe she should have been content where she was. Honestly, this man made her a little uncomfortable.

"Come over anytime. I'm still stocking the shelves. I lucked out and bought out a used bookstore online for a little bit of nothing. The books are being shipped in boxes, and I think they've mostly arrived."

"All right. I guess if any get misdirected this way, I'll know where to take them."

"Be sure to send some of your banana bread over with them."

"I'll do that," she said, giving him a smile, because he'd been kind to her, before he walked out.

She waited until he walked down the street before she walked over to the door and locked it.

Then she walked through the bakery, out the back, and sat down on the back step, looking at the peach trees where the little green fruit were growing under the drooping branches.

Grace had said this was one of her favorite spots when she was growing up, and Lauren had to agree. It was one of hers too. There were so many memories here. So many good times. So much fun with her mom.

Sure, there were times where she wished she would have had a dad, but her mom had said that she had gotten pregnant, and her boyfriend wanted her to have an abortion, while her mom had wanted to get married. They hadn't gotten married, but she hadn't gotten an abortion either, and her mom had moved out of town because it was a small town, and she didn't want to embarrass her family.

Growing up, from what she'd heard of her grandfather and grandmother, she didn't think that they were the kind of people who would have been embarrassed or at least who would have been upset and kicked their daughter out. But sometimes people got older and mellowed out. Regardless, they lived just south of Milwaukee, and Lauren only saw them once or twice a year.

It was hard to know someone when you only saw them once or twice a year. They had passed away, and her mom had grieved but had continued making ends meet.

In hindsight, Lauren admired that. How she could lose people in her life and just continue on with her life, like...like it didn't throw her through a major loop.

Well, that was one of the ways she and her mom were different. Although she didn't really have any direction in her life to continue on with. She was just drifting, so far from the husband she barely saw. Her purpose had been taking care of her mom. When that had ended, she didn't really know what to do with herself. Go back to teaching? She didn't really want to. She had enjoyed it but hadn't loved it the way she loved baking.

She breathed deep of the fresh lake air. She missed this. Cincinnati didn't smell the same at all and didn't feel the same either. Coming here had been the right thing to do.

Her phone buzzed, and she saw that her husband had texted her again.

His texts had started out casual, not panicked after he'd seen her note.

> Lauren, when are you coming home? I want to talk about this. That had been one of the first ones.

And then he sounded irritated.

> Lauren. Am I really going to have to take off work and come get you? Plus, how do I know you're okay? At least let me know you're okay.

At that point, she realized that she could have been abducted by someone and being held for ransom, and he wouldn't know.

And then, the one that just came in.

> Lauren, I'm on my way to my sister's house.
> If you're not there, you can save me some
> time and let me know where you are.

He was going to look for her? He was leaving his precious business? She looked at the time. It was three o'clock in the afternoon. Maybe he wasn't leaving his business, but he was definitely taking off early, which he never did. Well, he'd needed to take off early so he could go to her mom's funeral. He had tried to talk her into having it in the evening, but the best time had been in the afternoon so people could come and get back home if they wanted to. Plus, they were going to have a little graveside service, and she didn't want that to happen in the dark.

She had won, she supposed, although there really hadn't been an argument. He had capitulated pretty easily, although it had been obvious that he hadn't been happy about it, and she had seen him on his phone two or three times during the service.

She had been standing by the casket. He had stood in the back, until it was time to sit down. Then he had come and sat beside her.

She hadn't really felt like he was supporting her. She had felt like he was just there and couldn't wait to leave.

Still, he had driven her to the graveside service and stood beside her during it.

He had also helped make the arrangements. Which she should be thankful for.

She really hadn't been in any condition to do it, and she probably would have screwed it up anyway. As it was, he got a really good deal on the funeral. Or at least, that's what she understood from talking to other people, because they paid about half as much as what normal people paid.

But that was one of Cannon's fortes—he was good at knowing business owners, and he had a few who owed him favors. She would never have thought that having a funeral director on one's list of people who owed one favors would be a good thing, but it turned out to be not bad, she supposed. Still, she didn't care how much it cost. She had to bury her mom somehow.

A breeze shifted the trees overhead, and it was almost like her mom was beside her again. Or maybe waiting in the branches.

She missed her so much. Before she knew it, she was crying, hot tears streaming down her face, an empty feeling in her stomach, and a desperation to see her mom one more time and be able to talk to her almost driving her to the ground. Why? Why her? Why couldn't someone else lose their mom? Why did it have to be her?

But she knew the answer to that question, or rather, maybe a better question to ask would be, why not her? Why did she think she was special and shouldn't have to lose her mom?

She didn't have any answers.

Six

"Hey, Cannon. We've been expecting you." Philip, his brother-in-law, opened the door and stepped back so Cannon could go in.

Monique, his sister, walked over, a baby in each arm. "Cannon. You came to see your nieces finally."

"I did?" he murmured, and then he realized that he'd just told them he was coming, he hadn't mentioned why. "Right. They look cute," he said, looking at them and then back up at her.

"Where's Lauren?" she asked.

This was going to be more awkward than he anticipated. He had assumed that she would be here. After all, she and Monique had found out that they were expecting together. Twice now, they'd celebrated together and been so excited. And twice, Lauren had lost her baby, while Monique had had a son first and then twin daughters.

He just assumed that Lauren would want to go where the babies were. She was such a baby person.

She loved children. That's why she became a teacher. He didn't really understand the pull, but hey, if that's what his wife liked, he was okay with it.

"She's not here?" he asked, and he knew immediately that he had just opened a huge can of worms.

"She's not here. Was she supposed to be?" Philip had shut the door and came over and stood beside them.

"I just assumed she was."

"No, she's not."

Lonnie, the three-year-old son, zipped through the room, making truck noises and dodging around people and furniture and several toys that were strewn around.

"Watch the babies, son," Philip said in a tired voice that almost made Cannon laugh. If he hadn't been so concerned about his wife, he probably would have.

As it was, he couldn't figure out where in the world she would be. She must have gone to Raspberry Ridge. And he found himself irritated that he'd texted her, specifically asked her to let him know if she wasn't here, and she hadn't.

He just assumed that meant she was. And he'd figured he was pretty clever for figuring it out.

Now he didn't know what to do.

"Sit down. You can hold them. Are your hands clean?" Monique said while she kind of ushered him into a chair. He found himself going and sitting without even really thinking about it, and before he knew it, he had a twin in each arm.

They were so tiny, they looked so fragile, and they were ugly as sin.

Who in the world thought babies were cute?

Although, as he studied the one face, he could kinda see Monique in there. And to his surprise, he picked out a few features that looked like his brother-in-law too.

Wow. That seemed almost like a miracle.

It would be another miracle if the kids actually grew up looking halfway decent after starting out life looking the way they did. Their faces were all scrunched up, and they looked a little bit like monkeys. He could understand why people believed in evolution. Although, being in the security business, he knew that things were often not the way they seemed. And looks could be very, very deceiving.

But not Lauren. Lauren was as solid as a rock. How could she have left him?

"Quick, let me get my phone out and take a picture. I don't know if we'll ever get you to hold them again. We kept asking for a picture of you with Lonnie when he was a baby, and we never got another one."

"You have plenty of pictures of Lauren, and that was good enough for me." He loved looking at the pictures of his wife. His sister always sent them to him, every time Lauren went down to visit, and she always looked amazing to him. So alive, so happy, beaming with joy. It was always a nice break from taking care of her mom. He didn't mind the added expense of hiring someone to care for her mother while she was away for a day or two.

He'd always done right by her.

Except, sometimes she'd come back with the deep sadness that he wanted to be able to assuage but could never quite touch.

It wasn't his fault that they couldn't have a child. She'd lost three that he knew of. Maybe more. She just didn't seem to be able to carry them. But they kept trying. He enjoyed that part of course. He figured trying was the fun part. Actually raising the kid... He wasn't so sure about that. But he'd do it for Lauren, because he'd do anything for Lauren. And she knew it. Except...she'd left. And why?

"Hold still there," Philip said, sitting down in a comfortable recliner facing his brother-in-law and looking lovingly at his wife, who hovered a little bit by Cannon's elbow. He wouldn't mind if she took the kids back. The longer he held them, the more he was afraid he was going to do something to hurt them or drop them.

"She left the apartment, and I assumed that she came here."

"She didn't tell you where she was going?" Philip asked, his eyes narrowing with suspicion.

"She left a note?" Monique said, and she had the same suspicious look on her face that his brother-in-law had. Like he had done something wrong.

"She left a note, but it didn't say where she was going. And no. If I knew where she was, I wouldn't have shown up here."

"Do you think something happened to her? Do you think she had a car accident?"

"The police would have contacted me, wouldn't they? I'm her husband after all."

Just because she apparently was a little bit miffed at him didn't mean the police weren't going to call him if something happened to her. He was still her husband.

"I would assume so. Unless she asked them not to."

"Why would she do that? She's married to me." He felt irritated at this line of questioning. And he also felt antsy, like he'd messed up, and now he needed to run to Raspberry Ridge. But then, what if she wasn't there? What was he going to do then? Because those were the two places he knew to look for her. If he didn't find her there, he didn't know what he was going to do.

"Why did she leave you?" Monique asked, and only a sister could get away with a question like that. She didn't seem the slightest bit upset about asking him either. She asked like it was her right. "What did the note say?" she said when he took a second to answer.

"Not much. Just that she was leaving. She didn't seem mad. She just seemed..." She actually seemed lonely, now that he thought about it. He supposed he should have realized that she probably would be, with her mother being gone and all. Maybe he should have taken a couple of days off work and done something with her.

"She seemed?" Monique prompted when he trailed off.

"Sad. Probably sad would be the best word." He didn't want to say lonely. Because that made it look like he was doing something wrong. And how was he supposed to know that she needed him to be with her if she didn't say? After all, she had a mouth. She could talk.

But he knew that being married meant sometimes knowing things without being told. Or figuring things out. After all, the Bible did say that a man was to dwell with his wife according to knowledge. He knew it was his responsibility to have knowledge of his wife, and...as he thought about it, he might have shirked his duties a little bit, but for good cause, since he was trying to build his business.

For some reason, it reminded him of Saul when he had taken the cattle and herds that he wasn't supposed to, and when Samuel jumped him about it, he said that he was going to use it as a sacrifice. He tried to make it sound like he was doing a good thing, even when he knew he was doing something he wasn't supposed to.

That wasn't exactly the point of the passage, but it seemed to apply right now to him. He had been doing what he thought was a good thing, but he knew that he had shirked his duty.

Well, as soon as he got to her, he'd apologize, and Lauren would forgive him, because she always did, and that would be that.

"Do you want to take these babies? I keep thinking I'm gonna drop one."

"You know they have names," his sister said, moving down to grab one. "This one is Arianne, and this one is Mary Lou," she said as she expertly scooped the babies up. He figured they were six weeks or two months by now. Something like that. Lauren had come down and helped Monique for a few days after they'd been born, but her mother had been in such bad shape, she hadn't stayed long.

He'd figured she'd want to come back and spend more time with them. It made sense to him. But apparently he'd guessed wrong.

"I know. I just can't tell them apart. I can't believe you can."

"Sometimes we do have trouble. We always dress Arianne in green, and Mary Lou gets pink."

"That's hardly fair. I'd hate to be the one who's always dressed in pink," he said.

His sister let out a laugh. "Maybe you better worry about your wife rather than the color of baby clothes."

"Or the state of your marriage," Philip said softly, but Cannon heard.

"What's that supposed to mean?" he asked, shifting but not getting up. He was hoping that perhaps Monique had an idea of where his wife was. But he was going to have to take the grilling and the questioning if he wanted to find out what she knew.

"Just that you spend a lot of time on your business, and I think your wife felt neglected for a while."

"I don't think that's any of your business."

"It might not be our business, but it's the truth." Monique stood in front of him, a baby in each arm, looking at him with her older sister glare. "She's been through a really rough time. Not only did she lose three babies in the last three years, but she lost her mom as well. And you haven't really been around to comfort her."

"She didn't tell me she wanted comforting," he said, feeling justified but again remembering that he was making an excuse for something that he was supposed to have known. Sometimes a man just needed to figure some things out about his wife. And he could, if he put as much effort into his wife as he did into his business.

At least he wasn't golfing. He could have been putting all of his effort into improving his golf swing or playing racquetball with his buddies at the gym. Then he felt like she probably would have had a leg to stand on. But he'd been putting his effort into something good. Building a business for them so they would have money to do whatever they wanted to. Hire a nurse for her mother when she wanted to go visit babies, for example.

Monique's lips pressed together, and he could tell that she wasn't impressed with his answer, not that he expected her to be. It rang hollow to him too.

"Monique's right. Sometimes your wife needs you to do things without being asked. Those emotional things are some of those things. I'm sure she wouldn't hesitate to ask you to fix the toilet or take out the trash, but... Sometimes when she just needs you to hold her, you have to figure that out on your own. I kinda thought you were a little smarter than that." Philip didn't look like he hated him exactly, but he did look a little disgusted.

He didn't see any point in arguing, although Philip's words made him feel extremely defensive. He wanted to say that this wasn't his fault. That his wife should have stuck around. Should have talked to him about it at the very least, but he supposed this was kind of a hard thing to talk about, and he also supposed it was probably obvious. When someone lost their mother, they wanted comfort. And they didn't want to have to ask for it.

"I guess I see what you're saying." He put his head down and felt really humble as he asked the next question. "Do you guys have any idea where she might be?"

His words were soft and came out without any confidence behind them at all. He really didn't know, other than Raspberry Ridge, and he didn't want to drive the whole way there just to find out that he was still on a wild goose chase. He wanted to be with his wife. He wanted to find her, now. Make sure that she was okay. Fix things between them. It bothered him that they weren't okay.

"No. She hasn't called or texted us, and we honestly didn't know that she had left you."

To hear someone else say it made it sound really weird and real, and he hated that. He didn't want it to be real. He wanted to wake up and find out that it was all a dream.

"All right. Any ideas after that?" If there was anywhere he could stop and check along the way, he'd do it. Just so he kept all of the stones turned over. He didn't want to miss even one.

"I guess a couple of times she talked about going to Yellowstone. She said she'd always wanted to see Old Faithful. But beyond that, she talked about working at an orphanage in Romania. Something about holding babies that needed it. And I had told her that there were jobs in the NICU across America where she could work, holding babies. That seemed to be something she really wanted. To hold a baby."

Cannon couldn't feel worse if someone had kicked him right in the gut.

Of course. She wanted a baby. She had cried almost inconsolably all three times she'd miscarried, and he hadn't understood. After all, the baby was in heaven. It was safe. She'd see it someday. He didn't understand what the big deal was. But he should have tried harder to find out what her problem was, why she was so grief-stricken, and done more to help her. He'd really dropped the ball. In fact, he was feeling more and more like maybe he hadn't been the exemplary husband that he'd always thought he was. In fact, maybe he'd been a really rotten husband.

"You know, I think she loves you. In fact, I know she does. Sometimes I can't figure out why," Monique said with the honesty of an older sister. "But I think sometimes she just really wished for things you didn't provide. Like you always provided security. Of course."

Cannon almost snorted. That was his job. He should have been good at that.

"But empathy and compassion. Kindness, companionship. She spent a lot of time alone. I think that sometimes Lauren was an extrovert, and it was really hard for her to be alone. Even if she was an introvert, she would have needed attention from her husband. Even introverts don't want their husband to completely ignore them for days on end."

He wanted to defend himself again, but he didn't. She was right. There were times where he was so focused on bidding on a job or whether or not he had gotten another job and how he was going to do a thorough job on a project that had come in and he was afraid the bid was too low and he'd stressed out, and all those things together had kept his mind busy. He'd been home, but he hadn't really been home.

"All right. I suppose you're right. I... I'll think about that as I drive to Raspberry Ridge. Do me a favor, and if you think about where else she might be, let me know. I... I love her. I don't want to live without her."

It was hard to admit that. Especially when they knew that she had just walked away from him. Apparently as easily as that. Walking away. But it was the truth. And it was also maybe a little of what he needed. Humility. Because he wanted his wife, and whatever he needed to do to get her back, he would do.

There wasn't anything he wouldn't do for her.

Seven

Dawn had barely lightened the sky the next day as Lauren walked out of her house and headed toward the cliff toward the path that led to Pebble Beach.

This was her favorite time of day. She'd slept better than she had in a while, although still not well. And she figured getting up and taking a walk would be good for her mental state and her physical health.

Interestingly, as she walked down the trail, she heard footsteps behind her and turned to look.

The bookshop owner had already spotted her and waved as soon as she turned around.

He wore jogging shorts and a muscle shirt, seeming oblivious to the chill of the morning. Or maybe he anticipated warming up soon, as it looked like he was going for a jog.

"Hey there, neighbor. I didn't expect to see you here this morning. It's pretty early," he said as she debated about turning around and continuing on. She decided against it. It seemed rude, and she was almost certain they would not be going at the same pace, so she wasn't worried about having to spend her walk beside him.

"This is my favorite time of day," she said honestly, moving forward as soon as he had reached her. "I'm Lauren."

She didn't want to hang around talking to him any more than she had to. He seemed like a nice guy, but she wasn't looking for male friendships and definitely not with single men who seemed to be unattached and possibly looking. She was making an assumption there, but any man who looked that good was almost certainly used to having a woman on his arm, if not two or three.

She was not interested in a man who didn't know how to stay true to one woman.

One more check in the positive column for her husband. He might not have paid a whole lot of attention to her, but at least he'd been faithful. And she never worried about it. Because that's just the way he was. She didn't think he could manage two women at once. He'd say he could barely manage the woman he had, and while he meant it as a joke, it was very close to the truth.

Regardless, she wasn't here to think about Cannon either. She was here to...focus on the future, look on the bright side, train her brain to think about the good things, because she didn't want to be stuck in the sad and lonely and mourning loop forever. She wanted to get out of it.

"Matteo," he said, offering his name without offering his hand. "This is the best time to run. I'm from the south, and down there, if you don't run early, forget about it. After about eight o'clock, it's too hot to do anything."

"The South. Texas?" she asked, figuring that the South was a pretty big area.

"South Carolina. So, maybe not as hot as Texas. Although I spent my fair share of time there too."

He'd traveled. Interesting. She'd gone from here to Cincinnati and back. That was the extent of her traveling. That was something else that she'd always wanted to do, although she would have preferred to have children with her when she did it. She had been content to save their money and hold off on taking any trips until they had kids to go with them. But that didn't seem like something God was going to give them, and her husband wasn't the slightest bit interested in looking into adoption or anything else. At least, the few times she'd asked him, he had barely glanced up from his laptop.

"I'm from here, so I know the mornings can be quite chilly in every season but summer."

"But they're still your favorite?"

"I suppose they're my favorite from a nice warm room in my house during the winter and possibly the fall and the spring. But they're my favorite outside in the summer."

"All right. You did need to clarify."

They hit the bottom of the beach, and she nodded at his last comment, then he said, "I'll see you around later. Don't forget, I owe you a couple of books. Be sure to stop by."

"All right," she said, waving as he did a few stretches before he started jogging down the beach.

After thinking about it for a minute, she decided to walk north instead of south. Just to go in the opposite direction that he had. She didn't want to meet him again, and while she thought he was a nice guy, that wasn't why she'd come here.

Still, it was interesting that she had a handsome, single—if his bare wedding ring finger had anything to say about it—man next door. She, of course, wore her ring, and she assumed that the man had seen it and understood.

Putting that encounter out of her mind, she lifted her face to the light breeze, resisted a shiver, and started heading in the opposite direction as Matteo. It was a beautiful morning with a sunrise spreading all across the sky and making it glow with oranges and pinks and shades of blue and even green.

It was glorious, and it reminded her that God loved her still, even if it felt like she was going through a winter period of her life.

Maybe she should text her husband. At least let him know that she was okay. His last text had just asked simply,

Are you still alive?

She couldn't tell whether he was worried or not. He was probably so busy, he barely noticed she was gone.

A nagging voice said that she wasn't being very considerate.

She wanted to answer back that he hadn't been very considerate for a really long time. But the longer she walked, the more clearly she heard that voice. She would hate it if Cannon had done this to her. She would be frantic if she didn't know where he was and if he wasn't answering her texts. Frantic and furious when she found out that he was actually okay, reading her texts, and just dismissing her out of hand.

Why had she done this to him? She was a terrible person. Only terrible people made their loved ones worry like this.

That was assuming that Cannon was worried. But what she knew of him indicated that he probably wasn't worried, unless it had to do with his business. Still, by the time she'd walked a mile and a half and turned around, she felt guilty enough to pull her phone out of her pocket and send him a text.

I'm fine. Keep working.

Maybe that was a little bit of sarcasm. Maybe that was a little bit of her bitterness and anger coming out. But in a text, they would just be words, not dripping with eye rolls and a you-never-pay-attention-to-me, you-really-don't-care-about-me, I-feel-lost-in-this-marriage-like-I-don't-matter kind of attitude.

Her phone buzzed almost immediately.

Where are you?

She bit her lip. She hadn't wanted to start a conversation, she just felt guilty about him worrying about whether or not she was alive or dead.

She walked another half mile before she decided that she probably ought to answer him. As much as she didn't want to.

Don't worry about it. I'm fine. Didn't you see my note?

I saw it, but it didn't say where you were. Where are you?

She hadn't even gotten three steps in before his answer came back.

She didn't know her husband could text that fast.

Was he going to ask until she answered?

She pressed her lips together and then figured it wouldn't hurt. It wasn't like she was hiding from him. She just...didn't feel like he cared, and she supposed that since he'd asked at least five times where she was, maybe he did care a little. And she could hardly complain that he didn't care if she wouldn't answer his question.

> Raspberry Ridge, staying at my mom's bakery. I think I might open it again.

She looked at that one for a bit before she hit send. After all, that was more information than she had intended to give him.

> Come home. We can open a bakery in Cincinnati.

She had never, in all the years of marriage, done what she was about to do right now.

She typed two letters.

> No.

Anytime he had expressly asked her to do something, she always replied with yes. She had made it her mission to say yes to her husband for everything that she could. Her husband loved Jesus, and he loved her as well, and she knew he would never ask her to do anything that was wrong or immoral. He'd asked her to do plenty of things that she didn't want to at times, but because he was her husband, and because she had determined that she would always say yes to him, she'd done them. And she hadn't complained.

And he hadn't thanked her.

She wasn't even sure he'd noticed.

Well, he might be surprised at her answer, and then again, he might not. She wasn't sure, and she supposed it didn't matter. She had no intention of going back.

But wasn't that what she was supposed to do as a submissive, obedient wife? Just because she'd left him didn't mean that she wasn't supposed to follow the Bible's command.

She wanted to kick that thought out of her head. She also wanted to argue that he had not been a biblical husband and had not loved her as Christ loved the church and gave himself for it. He also had not dwelt with her according to knowledge, because he had made no effort to find out what she needed after her mother's death or after losing the babies. But there was no qualification on her command. It didn't say that she was to obey and be submissive as long as her husband treated her well. Or as long as her husband upheld his end of the bargain, or as long as her husband did anything. There was no "as long as her husband" in the Bible. The command was just that. A command...

So, knowing that, she made a decision that was very much unlike her.

She wasn't going to listen to what the Bible said. She was going to ignore that, and ignore her husband, and ignore the fact that she was supposed to be submissive and obedient. She wasn't going to put up with him.

Even as she made the decision, it made her exceptionally uncomfortable. This wasn't the right decision. She knew it, and yet...she didn't want to do anything else. That was the bottom line. She wanted to be happy. She wanted to have someone who cared about her, she wanted to feel safe and secure and...comforted. Just to have someone understand what she was going through.

Was that too much to ask?

She figured it probably was, but she wasn't going to think about it anymore. Because she didn't want to feel any more guilty than she already did. Instead, she looked at the beautiful sky, which had started to turn a deep, sober blue, and then looked out at the lake, which reflected the blue back. Lifting her head, breathing in the bracing, fresh lake air, she focused on what she planned to do that day.

Maybe she would go pick out a couple of books, and sit between the shady grove of peach trees, and read for the day.

Or maybe she should make some cheese bread and take that over and get several books instead of just a couple.

Man cannot live on bread alone, so she probably should take some money too. But she had a very limited supply of it, and she wasn't sure what her husband was going to do. So she didn't want to spend any more than what she'd saved from her teaching job years ago. After all, she didn't want him saying that she had pilfered money from his business in order to leave him and start her own.

Not that she thought her husband would say anything of the kind. He'd always given her money for whatever she needed. They had a shared checking account, and there was always at least four figures in it and sometimes five. She could spend it however she wanted to, and he wouldn't ask any questions. He was a very, very generous man.

One more point in his favor.

Maybe she was the one who was wrong.

Eight

"Thanks for your hospitality," Cannon said as he got ready to walk out the door. He had a mug of coffee in one hand, which his sister told him not to worry about returning—it was a tumbler. She'd grab it at his house the next time she was there. He knew she wouldn't hesitate to do that, and he needed the coffee. It was early, the sun was barely out.

"Let us know if you find her. I'm worried about her," Monique said, holding a baby in one arm and looking like she'd slept all of five minutes the night before.

Why did people want to do that to themselves? Babies made people miserable. And yet, Monique looked at her child with such love and affection in her eyes, and Philip looked at his wife and child in the exact same way.

What was he missing?

He hadn't managed a response when his phone buzzed.

It was probably his foreman, asking a question about the day, and he pulled it out.

To his surprise, Lauren's name came up.

"She's alive," he said.

"You should require a picture. Maybe it's just a kidnapper trying to fool you," Philip said.

Sometimes with Philip, Cannon couldn't figure out whether he was joking or not.

"I'm going to ask where she is. I'll let you know if I find anything out."

"All right. Have a safe trip," Monique said, giving him a hug with her free arm. He hugged her back, his coffee in one hand, waiting for Lauren to respond. It was taking forever.

He made it out to his truck and had the motor started before she finally told him that she was in Raspberry Ridge. At the shop that her mom had owned, and she was thinking about reopening it.

How could she? Their home was in Cincinnati? What was she doing in Raspberry Ridge?

Except...she had said that she was leaving him. She was lonely. And... he kept wanting to forget that.

He had the note tucked in his wallet so he could get it out and read it if he ever needed to be reminded. But he knew that she had been right. He had not been a very good husband, and neither Monique nor Philip had tried to disabuse him of that idea. Just that in itself said that obviously, this was all his fault.

So, he pointed his truck northwest. He was going to get to his wife today. It would be late, but he'd be there. And hopefully, she would talk to him. He didn't see why she wouldn't. Lauren was not an unreasonable person.

Just like he'd done every day since he'd found the note, which felt like ages ago but had only been a couple of days, he started praying and didn't stop until he had pulled into Raspberry Ridge.

Nine

"It was really nice of you to meet us," Grace said, standing up from the bench underneath the grove of trees and walking forward to wrap her arms around Lauren.

The other lady must be Claire. Lauren could kind of see the resemblance to her teenage friend.

She also stood and waited her turn to give Lauren a hug. Lauren hugged them both back, feeling like she had stepped back in time.

Why had she waited so long to reconnect with her friends?

But she knew why. The tragedy that lay between them had split them apart, even if the fault line hadn't been obvious at first. It was why they didn't get back together after high school, and they'd all gone their own separate ways, getting out of Raspberry Ridge just as fast as they possibly could.

"I'm sorry, I can't stay too long. I have my cheese bread rising."

"You're making cheese bread?" Grace said, her hands clasped to her chest. "We should lay siege to your shop later!"

"Are you opening it again?" Claire asked, her eyes lighting up at the prospect.

"I've thought about it, but... I don't really know if I can make a go of it, you know?"

"I guess that's the risk of being a business owner. That's why there's a big payoff. Versus just being an employee, you know?"

She nodded.

She supposed that was true. The risk, the amount of time it took that a person had to spend to baby their business along until it was big enough to grow on its own.

That's what Cannon had been busy doing. And what she had supported him in, for so long. It just got...old, when the business always took first place.

"Anyway. Enough about that. How have you been?" Grace asked, truly wanting to know.

"I guess I'm hanging in there. You know I lost my mom, we talked about that, and that's just been hard."

"Yeah. I was a little worried about you after seeing you yesterday. I'm so glad we were able to get together today."

"Me too. I just lost my gram, which I know is not the same thing, but it's still tough."

"Yeah. I'm sorry. I hadn't heard. She was such a sweet woman. I have so many good memories of hanging out at her farm and playing. I also remember that truth or dare game. You and Josiah. That kiss. He couldn't stop talking about it for months afterward."

"Well, I gotta say, he was a good kisser then, and he's even better now."

They laughed together, and Lauren honestly started to feel like she was coming home.

"I know that this is a hard time for you, but if you want to talk about what happened with Yolanda, Claire and I tried to hash it out, and—"

"No. I'm definitely not ready for that. Too many other things. And I don't care if I never talk about that again."

The other ladies nodded, but she got the feeling they disagreed with her. Maybe they were right. Maybe it was better to talk about things rather than hide them, but she always figured that there wasn't really a Bible verse for that. Maybe just sharing it with the Lord. And working through it that way. But to actually talk about it with other people... She didn't need to.

Still, maybe it wouldn't hurt. Maybe they would be able to say some things that would assuage her guilt. But she didn't want platitudes. She didn't want to not have guilt that she deserved to carry around. After all, she could have stopped the whole thing. And Yolanda would still be alive.

"That's totally up to you. No one can force you into it. Still, I feel better after talking to Claire about it." Grace spoke, and then she totally changed the subject. "I heard there's a new bookshop opening up right beside the bakery. That is fortuitous, isn't it?" she said, wiping her eyes and looking excited.

"I heard the guy that's opening it is retired military. I haven't actually seen him, but you know how gossip travels in this town."

"I've seen him. And I believe it. He looks like he worked in intel or something. His eyes scan constantly, and while he seems very laid-back, there is an alertness around him that's disconcerting at times." Lauren figured that was a safe subject.

Grace jumped on that immediately. "You've seen him?"

"Yeah. He said he followed his nose into the bakery yesterday when I was making Nutella banana bread."

"Oh my goodness. That stuff smells so good. I hope you open the bakery again. I miss walking down Main Street and just being able to follow my nose to some delightful treat."

"Well, none of this stuff is healthy. I feel like I would just be selling heart disease to my friends and neighbors, and I don't really want to do that."

"So make healthy twists on the favorites. Or sell healthy stuff along with the junk. Honestly, there's got to be some room for junk in our lives."

That's kind of what Matteo had said. Even though he didn't look like the kind of person who ate much junk.

"What about your husband? Is Cannon following you here? Or is he already here?" Claire asked.

"No. He's still in Cincinnati."

"Are you guys...separated?" Grace asked cautiously. Then she put a hand up. "You don't have to tell me if you don't want to. My husband cheated on me, and I divorced him. We didn't have any children, so that didn't complicate the situation."

"Mine cheated on me too. Only we did have children to complicate the situation, and we tried to work it out. He had an affair with our therapist. So, I guess his idea of working it out didn't jive with mine, so I came here. Lost, broken, and pretty sure that my life was basically over. I wanted to visit with my grandmother and feel safe again. And then she died."

"My goodness. You both had it rough."

"You know, it worked out for good. Because through it all, Josiah stood beside me. And while he wasn't really someone I was interested in in high school, he...was so strong and steadfast. So different than my husband, and, well, he was there for me. And my ex didn't want my kids for the entire summer, so they spent two weeks with him in Boston, and now they're back with me. So I pretty much have everything, except my loser husband, who I do not miss at all."

Claire looked particularly strong, and Lauren had to laugh.

"I think that's a pretty good ending," she said.

"Did your husband cheat on you? Because I feel like we're developing a theme here," Grace said, laughing. "Although, part of the theme is the second time around we find men who don't cheat. Because we're smarter."

"You know, that's one good thing about my husband. Actually, there's a lot of good things about my husband. Maybe I didn't appreciate him the way I should have. Because no. He didn't cheat. He's not a jerk. He's actually pretty nice. He's...maybe more of a doer rather than a talker, if that makes sense?"

"I think a lot of men are that way. They talk with the things that they do. Josiah's like that. He works with his hands a lot, and I think his love language must be acts of service, because anytime he wants to make me happy, he does a little improvement project around the house. That works for me," Claire said, laughing.

"Interesting," Lauren said. Maybe Cannon's love language was acts of service. She hadn't even thought about it. Was he trying to tell her he loved her by...working so much?

He insisted that he was working for her, and for them, but...she didn't really want him to work. She wanted his attention. She wanted his time. Was that a love language—time?

She'd skimmed through the book years and years ago, but she couldn't really remember. She remembered there was one that was words, and she thought that words were cheap. Words definitely weren't her love language.

She supposed they could be Cannon's, but she really wasn't sure. He didn't talk that much. So probably not.

"So he didn't cheat on you?" Grace said.

"You seem disappointed," Claire said, poking her with her elbow in the side.

"I do not. But it would have made a really cool club. Although," she looked at Lauren with sincerity, "I wouldn't wish that kind of pain on anyone. It was the worst year of my life, bar none. I guess I haven't lost my mother, so I suppose that could be worse."

"Yeah. Cancer was pretty bad. It's not an easy disease. And it wasn't fast, and there was a lot of suffering and pain and disappointment and... just general badness involved. Those last three years are mostly under a dark cloud for me. And I feel heavy when I think about them." She paused for a moment and then looked at the grove of trees around them. "I guess I still feel heavy. Sad. I wonder sometimes if I'm depressed?"

It was funny, she hadn't seen these ladies in years, and she'd just said something that she hadn't mentioned out loud to anyone.

"I think it would be perfectly normal for you to be depressed, after you lost your mother."

"I had three miscarriages too. I..."

"I'm so sorry," Grace said, standing up and coming over and putting an arm around her. She guided her to the bench, where they sat.

Claire followed suit, sitting down on the other side, until her friends, rather than facing her, sat beside her with their arms around her. Was this so hard? This is what she wanted her husband to do. To just sit there. And hold her, and tell her that he was sorry.

He hadn't managed to do it. Not once. He'd encouraged her instead to get off the couch and do something. That exercise made people feel better, and she needed to get out and walk around. And if she wanted him to, he could give her a job in the business. That would help her get around people, use some of her people skills.

She didn't want to resent him, but he just didn't know what she needed. And he hadn't asked. And to her shame, she hadn't told him.

"My husband... I know he cared. But he wasn't devastated the way I was. My sister-in-law, whom I love dearly, was pregnant the same time I was with my second miscarriage. She had a healthy baby boy. And it was about one month before my due date. It was hard. And then, three years later, right on my due date for my third miscarriage, she had a set of twins. That was pretty devastating, because it was right before my mom died."

"Wow. What timing."

"I know, right? And they were so happy. And I was happy for them. And I went down to help. The babies were adorable. I was thrilled I got to see them... I really was happy. But it was hard too. And then my mom died, and yeah. Things just spiraled from there, I guess. And now I'm here. And—"

"And your husband is not coming?" Claire asked gently.

"Probably not. I can't imagine he would leave his work for that amount of time. I haven't ever been able to get him to take off, and he kind of resented having to take off for my mom's funeral."

"You're kidding. That's terrible!" Claire said. It made Lauren feel better to hear someone sympathize with her, but at the same time, she felt like she needed to defend her husband.

"He really is serious about his business, and it paid for everything. I was able to quit my teaching job and just stay home and be a caretaker for my mom. And when I went for a couple days to help his sister with her new babies, we could afford to hire a nurse to take my place. I do really appreciate the fact that his business is successful. I just... I guess I'm jealous of his business. I feel like he didn't really cheat on me, but he definitely loves his business more than he loves me."

"I see. So that doesn't count as cheating, but it definitely counts as not being a good husband."

"Yeah. And I guess I'm not a good wife, because he told me he wanted me to come home and I told him no."

"That's understandable too," Claire said, squeezing her with the arm that was around her.

Somehow, just talking to her friends made her feel better. They didn't have any advice for her, and they certainly couldn't fix her circumstances, but just knowing that they cared made her not feel so alone.

It's what she needed from her husband. To feel like he cared. To feel like he was willing to put time in to show her that he cared. To act like he wanted to help her feel better, and that time away from his business wasn't upsetting or annoying to him.

"I think this happens with a lot of couples. You just grow apart, and no one says anything," Claire said.

"Yeah. Although, it seems like he knew that he wasn't paying a lot of attention to her and he expected her to just accept it, as that's what needed to happen in order for his business to take off."

"Yeah. That's pretty much it," Lauren said.

They sat there for a little bit longer, both Grace and Claire talking a little bit more about what was going on in their lives, and finally Lauren had to interrupt.

"I'm sorry, but I really do need to get back to my bread. It's going to rise up all over the place, and I'm going to have a mess on my hands if I don't get it in the oven."

"I might feel the need to stop by later," Grace said with a wink as they stood together.

"I'm feeling that same need," Claire said. "Probably in an hour or so, about the time the bread comes out of the oven."

"You ladies are welcome to stop by anytime."

"And if you need someone to help you get your store open, let me know. I would love to be able to come over and lend a hand, especially if you need any painting or decorating. You know that's my thing. And my husband is pretty handy with wood and stuff, and I know he'd be willing to give you a hand as well."

"My husband is a fix-it guy, and we're the same. You can pay us with food. I've been working on bread recipes on my own, although I haven't branched out to cheese bread yet. I guess I just don't think I could stand the disappointment when it doesn't taste like your mom's."

"I don't think anything would taste as good as hers, although cheese bread was my thing, so maybe."

"I think I'll have to taste and tell you," Claire joked as they started walking out.

They chatted a bit about the things that they missed about her mom's baked goods shop until they reached the end of the healing garden, and Claire headed toward her car after embracing Lauren and telling her that she'd love to get together anytime.

Grace gave her a hug as well. "I'm supposed to meet my husband on the beach, so I'm going to head that way. But I'm the same as Claire. Hit me up anytime you need someone to talk to."

They parted, and Lauren found herself almost smiling as she walked back to the bakery.

Ten

Cannon couldn't remember the last time he had been in Raspberry Ridge. It was a quaint town, cute, quiet. He could see why Lauren liked it here. Especially after losing her mom and the babies. If she needed a place to decompress, this little lakeside town was perfect.

And Lauren probably knew some of the residents, who were here when she was growing up.

Even while these things made sense to Cannon, he felt an urgent need to get back to Cincinnati. His business needed him. He didn't want to stay here. He definitely couldn't run a business here. There weren't enough customers to keep him solvent. He wondered if Lauren would be able to even keep a bakeshop solvent, but he knew her mom had run hers for years out of the little shop on Main Street.

He found a parking place not far from where it was. He'd been here a few times to visit her mom, but they didn't stay long. And it hadn't been recently. He hadn't wanted to leave his business.

Getting out of his truck, he noticed that there was movement behind the reflections in the window. Was she open already? He didn't see any open sign, and while the windows looked clean, there were no special signs or any other kind of paraphernalia advertising the day's offerings.

He thought about knocking but then figured he might as well try the door. If it was open, it'd be weird not to walk in.

The knob turned when he tried it, and so he pushed it open.

It took him a minute to register what he was seeing, as laughter hit him immediately. His wife's laughter.

When was the last time he'd heard that?

She stood at the counter, her elbows on it, a piece of bread with a huge bite taken out in front of her face as she chewed with her cheeks puffed out.

There was a man, like a military-type guy, standing across from her, holding the same kind of bread with several bites taken out, with his mouth full as well.

They had been laughing together, and now they were eating together, leaning over the counter facing each other.

He had been sure that his wife wasn't having an affair. She just wasn't that kind of person. But then, he suddenly remembered how many people he'd talked to whose spouse had had an affair, and they had said the exact same thing. They just weren't that kind of person. They never suspected anything. They had no idea. It had blindsided them. No one got married thinking that their spouse was a cheater.

But the fact that she was standing in such a cozy position, eating bread and laughing with a man who... Cannon wasn't exactly a good judge, but he figured he was the kind of man women were attracted to. He looked ruggedly handsome, and he wore a T-shirt that was about six sizes too small so all of his bulging muscles stood out. It definitely looked like he didn't miss too many days at the gym.

Cannon didn't have time to go to the gym. He was busy building a successful business. This dude had great muscles, but he probably didn't have the smarts or the drive to build anything himself. He was an employee somewhere. Probably for a delivery company or something that didn't take a whole lot of brains to do. Or require a lot of overtime, since the dude had time to spend a couple hours at the gym every day.

"Cannon!" his wife said, her word partially obscured by food in her mouth.

He narrowed his eyes. "Doesn't look like you were expecting me." He tried not to be nasty. Their relationship had never been nasty. He wasn't sure they'd ever even fought. Argued, sure. But a screaming match? He couldn't even imagine Lauren getting upset enough to scream at him. She just wasn't that kind of person.

Of course, he didn't think she was the kind of person to cheat either.

This might not be what it looks like. Calm down, dude.

His little pep talk didn't work a whole lot, but it did keep anything else nasty from coming out of his mouth.

"Why would I be?" she asked, and to his surprise, she looked defensive and even...angry.

Wait. He was the one who was angry here. She was the one who had left, not told him where she was going, sent him in the exact opposite direction to find her, wasted an entire day, and now he walked in and she was with some other dude, laughing her head off and acting all cozy like she hadn't acted with him in a long time. Years.

She'd left him under the impression that she was still grieving her mom and sad about her miscarriages. But apparently she wasn't that sad. Because she had just been laughing like she was eighteen with no cares in the world.

"Because you left without telling me where you were going. Because I wanted to know where you were. What did you think I was going to do? Just leave you? Without knowing whether you were safe or not?" He couldn't even believe that she wouldn't have known he was going to be showing up. Why did she think he'd wanted to know where she was so bad?

"I'm Matteo. I own the bookshop right beside here." The man pushed back from the counter, still holding some type of bread in his hand, and came forward with his other hand out.

Cannon looked at it but didn't take it.

"I suppose you probably need to get back to your business," he said instead, leveling a gaze at the guy.

"I'm sorry, Matteo. My husband is usually more polite." And to his consternation, Lauren came around the counter, holding something in her hand for Matteo. "Here's the bread I promised you. Thanks for stopping by. I appreciate the laugh. And don't forget about those books you owe me. I think it's up to about five or six now."

He grinned, and Cannon figured it was an engaging grin, because his wife smiled back. Which made Cannon even angrier. How dare she smile at this flirty, irresponsible gym rat and not give her husband a proper greeting?

He ground his teeth together but didn't say anything as Matteo took the wrapped bread Lauren handed him.

"Thanks. This is the best—I don't think I've ever had cheese bread before. This stuff is addicting."

They smiled at each other again before Matteo turned, glancing at Cannon and nodding his head.

Cannon ignored him as the man brushed past and walked out the door. The bell jingled as he left, and then it was quiet in the bakery.

Lauren turned on him, anger radiating from every pore, her eyes narrowed, her hands on her hips. "How dare you be so rude to my friend?" she said, and he had to blink in surprise.

She was angry? He couldn't believe it. He was the one who had every right to be angry, and she was the one attacking him?

But then he remembered. She was the one who had left. He was coming here to get her back. If he stood and fought with her, he wasn't going to convince her of anything.

"Friend?" he said instead, his brows lifted. They didn't look like they were just friends. They looked like they were a lot more.

"Yes. My friend. He's a business owner beside me. I'm in a town by myself with no family here. It's good for me to have friends. People who will help me if I need it. Who will make the time to stop what they're doing and come give me a hand. Just like I would do for them. It's a reciprocal relationship. Friends."

She said it like she was making some point at him, like he wasn't as good as Matteo. Obviously, some dude who had some dinky little shop in the middle of nowhere couldn't hold a candle to the multimillion-dollar business that Cannon had built over the last ten years. Why was Lauren attacking him with her hands on her hips, spitting out garbage like this dude was some kind of knight in shining armor?

"You haven't laughed with me like that in a long time," he finally said. If he wanted this to get straightened out, he couldn't fight over stupid stuff. He had to pick the things that were important. The problem was, he wasn't entirely sure what that was.

"You haven't made the time to stop what you were doing in the middle of the day and come over just so that you could stand across the counter and talk to me." She said the words without smiling and then lifted her chin, like she was getting ready to take a hit from him.

Why would she do that? He wasn't a hitter. She'd never had to worry about that. Why was she acting like he was? Maybe she was expecting a verbal hit. Or...maybe she was being defensive, and it was just a natural movement.

He tried to think about her words. He had wanted her to tell him what the problem was, and...maybe she was, and he was just missing it.

What was her accusation?

That he hadn't made time to stop to talk to her in the middle of the day.

Was that right?

"If you would have told me that you wanted me to stop working in the middle of the day, I could have stopped what I was doing, driven home, just so we could talk, if that's what you wanted."

She huffed out her breath and shook her head, closing her eyes.

Then she opened them and looked right at him. "I didn't have to tell Matteo what I wanted. He just did it."

She turned and walked back around the counter. There was a loaf of bread there that was cut. She pulled plastic wrap out of the drawer and then said, "Would you like a piece of cheese bread?"

He was about ready to say no, he didn't want to eat anything, he wanted to get this settled, when he thought that...maybe eating with her was what she wanted.

How did Matteo know to do the right thing? And he, who was married to her, couldn't seem to get it together? Didn't she appreciate the time and effort he was putting into the business he'd built for them?

"Yes, please," he said, wanting to say so many other things. A railing accusation for one. Telling her all the things that she was doing wrong. But she wasn't the one who'd chased him across the country. It was him who'd chased her. If he'd chased her, only to yell at her and tell her how terrible she was, he wasn't really doing himself any favors, was he?

He needed to keep himself calm and see if she would talk to him.

"Sorry I didn't stop work in the middle of the day and come talk to you..." Then he realized it was the middle of the day and he was here. "Except... I'm here now. Is it too late?"

He did not want to ask the question. He did not mean for it to come out of his mouth. He did not want her to say yes, it's too late.

But she didn't. She didn't answer him at all. Instead, she cut him a slice of bread, slathered a big pat of butter on it, which started to melt immediately, and then pushed it across the counter to where he stood, right where Matteo had stood just a few minutes before.

"Here you go," she said, but there was no smile or friendliness in her words. It was almost like she had pulled in on herself, trying to defend herself from him.

"Thanks." He took the bread, picking it up. But before he took a bite, he said, "Would you... Would you please tell me what I did wrong?"

He had as much humility in his voice as he possibly could. And suddenly, after the words were out of his mouth, he didn't want to have anything in his hand to eat. He just wanted to focus on his wife and listen to her.

If he was going to fix this, he needed to know exactly what he needed to do. A roadmap. Someone to say, stop work in the middle of the day, go talk to your wife, stand across the counter, so that she doesn't have to do it with some other man, instead.

"You know exactly what you did wrong," she said dismissively, not even looking at him as she ripped off the plastic wrap and set the bread on top of it.

"I promise you, I don't."

"You're a smart man. You can figure it out."

"Is it too late?" he said, and again, he wished he wouldn't have said it. He didn't want her answer to be yes. What was he going to do if she said yes?

"I suppose that's your decision. I'm here now, and I'm not going back to Cincinnati."

He blinked. "What?"

He'd thought they would just work it out, and she would come home. Maybe she was getting this ready to sell, except...hadn't she told him that she was going to open it again? Surely she wasn't serious.

"You heard me." She turned with the loaf of bread and stuck it on the far counter, then she started tidying up the area where she had been working.

"Lauren?"

She looked up, but her hands continued to move across the counter, wiping up the crumbs. She just lifted her brow.

"Would you talk to me please?"

He needed to know. Needed to have some kind of clue as to what he had to do.

"Now you want to talk? So all I had to do was come to Raspberry Ridge in order to get you to want to talk to me?" She rolled her eyes and then looked back down at the counter.

"Yeah. That was all you had to do. I'm here, now I want to talk. Please?" He knew that there was desperation in his voice, but he couldn't help it. It was almost like she was dismissing him, but he truly, truly did not know what he needed to do. How did he get his wife back? He didn't want to...go back to Cincinnati without her. He didn't want to go anywhere without her. He loved her.

"I'm busy. I'm putting my time and effort into my business. After all, I want it to be successful." There was something off about her words. She looked sincere, but was that sarcasm? Was that accusation? Why did her words sound...?

"I noticed there was no security system on the door. If you're going to live here, you need to have something."

"This is Raspberry Ridge. I don't really need to lock the door at night if I don't feel like it."

"You do. Don't you dare go to bed without locking the door." He tried to modulate his tone. She didn't understand all the stories that he'd heard about people getting broken into, almost murdered, and, in some cases, beaten up, raped, and shot. "It might be a small town, and you might feel safe, but that's when you let your guard down, and the bad people get in. You absolutely need to have a security system here."

"I'll get right on that," she said, taking the crumbs that she had wiped up and shaking the rag over the sink. "Now, if you don't mind, I'm closed."

"You're closed?" he said, wondering what she was trying to say. Was she...dismissing him?

"I might be open again. I might be open tomorrow, but for now, you need to leave so I can lock the door behind you." She gave him a tight smile and then walked out from behind the counter and stood by the door, her hand on the knob like she was going to open it for him.

He'd kind of trailed after her, and when he got beside her, she opened the door, a brow raised. Her expression said she was waiting for him to leave.

"Lauren. Please. I... I know I must have screwed up big time, but I'm having trouble seeing it. I worked hard to make our business successful so that it would support us and make money for us. I paid for a nurse to help you when your mom—"

She waved a hand. "Yeah. I know. Thank you. I probably didn't appreciate that like I should have. I'm tired, and I have a headache. I'll see you tomorrow."

He stood staring at her, the pain that he had allowed himself to feel ever since he'd found her note making his chest feel like it had been crushed, run over by something hard and heavy.

"We can talk tomorrow?"

She lifted her shoulder. "Sure. Tomorrow."

"All right." He stood uncertainly. Where was he going to stay? Raspberry Ridge wasn't even big enough to have a gas station, let alone a hotel. There was no place. And it didn't look like he was welcome to stay with her. In fact, he would say quite the opposite. She was clearly telling him he was not welcome.

He supposed he'd sleep in his truck. Although, he wasn't just giving her a hard time about the security system for this place, his truck was hardly secure or safe. But he was different than Lauren. He was a man. Women were targets because of their gender—solely because of their gender. Men were a little bit safer in that regard.

Plus, someone probably wasn't going to break the window of his truck just to steal it in this little town. But just like he had told Lauren, it was when a person let their guard down that bad things happened.

Still, he didn't have a choice. He walked out the door, wishing he had some kind of wise, compelling last words that would make her change her mind and ask him to stay, but no such words came to his head, and the door closed behind him. He could hear the lock turn and click into its place.

And then, like that wasn't bad enough, she pulled the shade down so he couldn't even look in the glass.

There were still two big windows on either side of the door, but he didn't try to look in those either. He'd gotten her message, loud and clear.

He started walking up the street, his mind whirling, his heart heavy and hard, chewing absently on his bread.

He thought maybe she really had intended to leave him. She had intended to walk out. And why? What had he done? Was there anything he could do to fix it?

She kept mentioning his business, and time, like that was an issue, but he really didn't know.

He got to the end of the street, finishing his bread when he saw the sign for a healing garden.

He'd never heard of such a thing, but he saw a bench inside and figured he could sit down for a while. Although, he was more likely to pace. Still, he opened the gate and went in, intending to sit at the first bench, but the garden was so peaceful, so beautiful, so compelling, that he kept walking. He went by a waterfall-type area where the sound of the soothing water almost made him stop at that bench, but somehow he continued on until he got to a shady grove of trees, on either side of the path, that shaded the path and felt so peaceful and welcoming that he walked to the bench and sat down, his forearms on his knees, holding his head in his hands.

What had he done? And what was he going to do to make it right? Was there anything he could do to make it right?

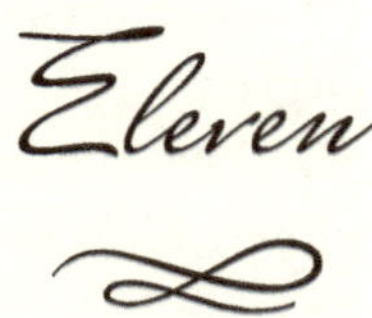

Eleven

Lauren hadn't been joking about having a headache. She put a hand to her temple and tried to think about whether or not there were any pain relievers in her purse.

Finally deciding she might as well look, she almost sighed with relief when she found a bottle of something that would work, shook two into her palm, and grabbed a glass of water to swallow them down with.

It was going to take a few minutes before the pain went away, and so she turned, walked through the back of the building, and went out and sat down on the steps.

A dog that she'd seen earlier, scrappy brown with white paws and a white collar, slunk out through the peach trees as she came out.

She should have come out slower. She'd seen it a couple of times before and knew it hung around. She'd left a couple of scraps out the night before, not that she had a whole lot to eat herself, but they'd been gone in the morning.

Still, she didn't want to think about the dog right now. She was just so mad at her husband. How could he be so smart and yet so dumb at the same time? Acting like he didn't know why she'd left. Like he wanted to make things right, but he wanted her to go home and for everything to just stay the same. He didn't want to have to actually put any effort into their relationship. He wanted that to just go smoothly so he could put all of his effort into his stupid business. And that crock about it being for both of them. And then he'd given her a guilt trip about how he'd paid for a nurse so she could leave her mom and go see the babies.

She rolled her eyes, which made her head hurt worse, so she leaned back over, putting her hands around her stomach and rocking forward.

He was infuriating. He absolutely refused to see what was right in front of his face and kept asking dumb questions. Plus, all of a sudden he wanted to talk? That was suspicious. He hadn't wanted to talk for the last ten years, just content to have her there, cleaning his house, cooking his meals, occasionally helping him in the business, whatever he needed, she was there. And yet, he never lifted a finger to do anything for her.

Okay. She was being unfair, and she was ranting. He had done things for her. Just not the things she really needed.

"There you are. The door was locked, and I thought that maybe you'd gone somewhere, but your car's sitting out front, so I came around back to see if you were here."

"Sorry, Skyler." She didn't explain about her headache or her husband or how infuriated she'd been with him. That was way too long a story. And she'd just met Skyler the day before when Skyler had stopped in and invited her to Bible study.

"Is it okay if I sit down?" She paused. "If you want to be left alone, that's fine too."

"No. You can sit down. I'm just so...angry."

"Oh. You don't look angry. When I get angry, my face gets all red, and people know that they better steer far clear of me. Of course, it doesn't happen often, but when it does, unfortunately, it's quite a spectacle."

Skyler's cheerful words made Lauren laugh. "I can just imagine. Actually, I can't. You're so cheerful. I would guess you would never get angry."

"Sometimes my husband is infuriating."

"Funny you should mention it. That's what I'm angry about. My husband, who has ignored me for literally a decade, showed up today and wanted to talk. Really? Talk. Now?"

"So I take it that...he followed you here?"

"Yeah. I'm sorry. I shouldn't unload on you. You don't need all my garbage."

"Actually, my life has been pretty smooth sailing lately. If you'd like to give me your garbage, I think I have room for it right now."

She chuckled a little at the way Skyler said it.

Maybe the fact that Skyler had sat down beside her, and she didn't have to face her, made it a little easier, but the invitation, and the desire to vent, won over her more reticent nature of not wanting to air all of her dirty laundry. It was a small town. People were going to know her husband had stopped in, people would probably even know that her husband had caught her laughing with Matteo and had gotten...jealous? Was that what the word was? She thought more that he was upset because she wasn't home, and he was inconvenienced having to go find her, but maybe that was wrong.

"Well, it's kind of a long story," she finally said, figuring that Skyler might not have stopped in for a long time.

"I'm down for a long story. Although, I kept smelling this really good scent, like fresh-baked bread, while I was working in my garden, so I thought I would take a stroll and see if I could find out who was making it. Matteo told me that it was coming from you, but...your door was locked. So, maybe that's why I ended up coming around. I'll do pretty much anything for fresh-baked bread."

It was hard to resist Skyler's cheerful friendliness.

"How about we go back inside, and I'll cut you a piece. Then, if you still want to hang around, I'll feel a little better for dumping on you."

And maybe, just cutting the bread and chatting with a stranger who was fast becoming a friend would ease her anger and make it so that she was chatting more than venting.

"I am not going to turn down that offer," she said. "I think Matteo said that it might have been cheese bread, and you know how small towns are. I've heard that the cheese bread that comes out of this place is divine." The way Skyler said "divine" made Lauren laugh again.

"I'm sure it's not heavenly, exactly. But it is one of the things I do best." She stood up from the step and held the door for Skyler to step through. "Just go straight."

"All right. I've never been back here."

"Yeah, there's a stairway here, and the steps go upstairs to my apartment, which is small."

She almost said to her mom's apartment, but while Skyler probably knew her mom, she wasn't sure, and she didn't want to get into that right now. That was something else that was still a little raw and hurt.

"I sure hope you're going to open this. You know how nice it would be to have a bakery in town?"

"It would be nice having a gas station and restaurant too, and maybe we're getting a hotel, right?" Lauren said, repeating the gossip she'd heard and raising her eyebrows in question.

"Yeah. All of those would be really nice. But the bakery's a good start," she said, staying on that side of the counter as Lauren went in and grabbed the bread that she had just wrapped up. It didn't take her any time at all to slice a nice thick piece off, and it was still warm enough to melt the butter.

"Thanks. Wow. That smells amazing, and it's still warm!"

"I think you've talked me into another piece," she said, although... She kind of lost her appetite after dealing with her husband.

"Oh my goodness, it tastes as good as you would think it would," Skyler said after taking a bite and humming a bit.

It was so nice to watch people enjoy something that she had made. And take such pleasure in it. Whether or not she could run a bakery, she still hadn't decided, but whether or not she wanted to was less and less of a question. She loved making people happy. Giving them something to smile about.

Even giving them a place to come and talk. To have her neighbors come to her, and exchange some laughter and fun, and become friends. It knitted a community together, and she almost felt like it was a necessity.

"So. You said something about your husband finally wanting to talk. Like, he hasn't before?"

"All right. But I'm warning you, this could take a while. You might want to sit down on that stool."

Skyler settled herself obediently, and Lauren moved the knife in her hand, remembering that she was going to spread butter on a piece for herself.

"My husband's a good man. He didn't cheat on me or anything like that. He's faithful and honest, he's got character. And honestly, he is... perfect." She paused. "Almost."

"I guess no one's perfect. But almost perfect sounds pretty good to me."

"Yeah. I guess... I guess it started with this business that he started. At first, I was on board, completely. But starting a business means lots of hours, no one else can do it, and you don't have the money to pay to hire someone to come in, so you do everything yourself. And I didn't mind. I helped him a lot too. But then, my mom got sick with cancer, and we moved her in with us so I could take care of her. I...got pregnant but then lost several babies in miscarriages. And...Cannon just kept working. When my mom had downturns, he just kept working. When Mom had a good doctor's appointment, Cannon was working. When I had another miscarriage, just before my mom died, Cannon was working. He...didn't take the time to give me what I needed. Someone to talk to. Someone to hold me. Someone to share the burden."

Skyler nodded sympathetically. But didn't say anything. She munched contentedly on her bread, but it was obvious from the way she looked and reacted that she was listening intently. Lauren told herself that she wanted to be just as good a listener as what Skyler was. She felt seen and heard and valued.

"Anyway. Mom died, and I was rattling around that old apartment by myself. And we have plenty of money, but I have no babies, I have no husband, because he's working all the time. And I know. I should be happy that he's working and not out playing somewhere. I suppose he could be at the gym for three hours a day, or he could be trying to be a professional cyclist and biking all the time. Or... I don't know. Just anything that men do that takes them away from their wives. At least he's making money with his obsession."

"Good point. He could be doing something that cost money. And ignoring you at the same time. That would be even worse."

"Yeah. You're right. So, what I mean is I wasn't mad at him exactly, I just...didn't feel married. I didn't have a partner. I didn't have someone who wanted to be with me. If he had a choice, he'd choose work over me every time."

"A woman wants to feel special. She wants to feel like she's the most important thing after God."

"Yeah. I guess if he were a preacher... Although, I suppose preachers could probably get obsessed by work and put their family in second place. It's not something that preachers would be immune to, I suppose."

"I think you're right. Preachers can be just as human as anyone else. And it's hard for a preacher to put his family first, because he has a whole congregation of people who are expecting him to drop everything when they need him, who have hired him to be there when they need him. His wife doesn't pay him."

"That's a good point." Lauren had never really thought about it that way.

"Oh yeah, it could be worse."

"I know. He could be out playing, or spending money, or addicted to porn, I guess, rather than working hard. Still, you're right. I didn't feel special. I didn't feel important. I felt like everything and everyone was more important than me, and it would take an act of God to get him away from work and to want to spend time with me." She lifted a hand and laughed without humor. "It actually did. I had to leave him before he actually took time off work to spend time with me. That's pathetic."

Skyler nodded as she listened. "That's hard. Why couldn't he have given you his time before? If he was going to take off work, why couldn't he have done it just to keep your marriage healthy? Why did he have to wait until it was on life support before he came, and... Was he apologetic?"

"He claims he has no idea what the problem is. He wanted me to talk to him. To tell him what was wrong. I mean, how could he not know?" She shook her head. "He just acted so dumb. And he is a smart man. I mean, he's really smart. And yet, he just doesn't know anything important."

"Anything about relationships. Maybe that's why God matched

men up with women. Because men have no clue about relationships, and they have a tendency to be smart about things that women, in general, aren't as good at."

"Yeah. He came in and criticized the fact that I didn't have a security system on my store. Like I have money for that." She rolled her eyes. "He knows how much they cost. He sells them and installs them for a living."

"No wonder he was worried about you. But...that says he cares, doesn't it?"

"I guess it does. I suppose. But he didn't take time for me. That says more than anything that he doesn't care."

"Sounds to me like your love language is quality time."

"I remember reading that book, but I don't remember what my language was, or his either, for that matter."

"I guess it doesn't really matter, except...sometimes when our love language is one thing, we miss someone talking to us in another language."

"What do you mean? They're all English."

"Or whatever language you're using. It's not a matter of a cultural language, it's... Someone who has a love language of quality time might not see the acts of service that her partner is doing for her because that's not her love language."

Lauren was quiet for a moment. That made complete and total sense and was almost like a part of the picture had come into sharp focus all of a sudden. Cannon maybe didn't spend time with her, not because he didn't love her, but because that didn't say "I love you" to him. To him, acts of service said "I love you," so he worked hard on his business to provide for her and made sure that their apartment was fixed up, and the oil changed in her car, and that type of thing.

She supposed if she thought about it, she could think of a hundred little things that he had done that, while she had appreciated them, she hadn't really thought they said "I love you."

"I think I see what you're saying," she said, though she really didn't want to. She wanted everything to be his fault. If she were being honest, she wanted him to be the bad guy. Maybe her opinion was biased and she needed someone who could see areas where she could do better.

She took a breath. She didn't really want to see where she could do better. She wanted her husband to change, not her. After all, he was the one who had neglected her and hadn't given her the support and care that she needed.

But he was here, in Raspberry Ridge, taking off work and apparently coming back tomorrow to talk to her, since she wouldn't do it today. She honestly thought if she'd refused to talk, he'd get in his truck and drive back to Cincinnati. After all, how was his business surviving without him?

Twelve

She swallowed and then looked carefully at Skyler. "Is there something I'm missing?" She blew out a breath and then said, "I'm not sure I can take a hard critique, but...other than the love languages, which you have a point on, I wondered if maybe there's more?"

It was hard to say that. She wanted to be just fine and make it so that if there was going to be any kind of reconciliation, she could make Cannon do it all.

"Well, I see that you have excellent points. Your husband should pay attention to you. He should note that when hard things happen to you, you need him to come and just put his arm around you and hold you and help you, even if it takes days or weeks or months for you to feel better. He can't just go work and expect you to...take care of yourself. Ideally. But... I guess I think about it like this. God tells us that He will give us everything we need. So for me to say that I need my husband to do this or I need my husband to do that for me, it can't be true, right? If God promises to supply all of our needs, and that 'need' of mine isn't being met, then it must not be a need, right?"

Ouch. And ouch again. Her headache was gone, but she just felt like she'd gotten her toe stomped on. Because she had been saying all along that her husband wasn't meeting her needs. But she could hardly argue with that statement, taken straight from the Bible. The Bible did clearly say that God would supply all of our needs. Why was she expecting her husband to do it?

Because that's what marriage was. It was when a man and woman got together, and the woman helped the man, and the man was there when the woman needed him.

Wasn't she there when Cannon needed her?

She felt like she was, but maybe he didn't think she was. Or maybe he was fine with it. And didn't understand why she wasn't fine too. Because his needs weren't that great. She tried to make sure there was food on the table when he got home from work, and she kept his house clean and helped him in his business if he needed it.

"All right. I'll give you that point. I can't think of a verse in the Bible to counter what you said. God does promise to supply all of our needs. Maybe I was depending a little too hard on my husband, expecting him to do things that he wasn't necessarily supposed to do. But was it too much for me to expect him to spend some time with me? To put his wife ahead of his business, even once in a while? Or to put his arm around me and console me in my grief?"

"Did you ever tell him what you wanted?"

"My husband is a very smart man." She knew what his grades had been in college, he had graduated at the top of his class in high school. His SAT score was almost perfect, and his IQ was genius level.

"Okay. So he can take a test. Good for him." Skyler lifted her shoulder. "I made a lot of mistakes when I was younger," she started.

Lauren perked up. She thought they were talking about her and her husband, but Skyler was going off in this direction. She settled in, taking another bite of her bread, and listened, trying to listen to Skyler the way Skyler had listened to her.

"I was on the streets, I guess. I wouldn't have called myself dumb, but I had a lot of street smarts. I still do. Just because of the environment I grew up in and the things that happened to me. My husband, Homer, is a very smart man. He works in computer programming, and no one would think he's any kind of intellectual slouch. But there are just some things that he doesn't know, because he hasn't experienced them. I wouldn't call him dumb, I just call him…

unaware. So there's that, when you haven't encountered something, and you haven't learned."

"I guess that could apply to my husband. But when I say he's smart, I guess I mean that in his business, he can figure out whatever he needs. Why can't he figure out what he needs to do for his marriage?"

"I think sometimes men don't realize they need to. They think that women are just like men. They think...they have good intentions, they want to have a good relationship, and everything seems like it's smooth sailing, so it's not crying out for attention, so they don't give their relationship attention. They put their attention somewhere else and think they're doing a good thing. Maybe... Maybe they don't need a whole lot of attention from their wife. Or maybe they're getting everything that they want. I don't know. I just know that men can be really smart when it comes to book learning and figuring out complicated analytical ideas, but when it comes to relationships, it's like there should be a whole other level to measure intelligence in that area, because a man's ability to be good at relationships has nothing to do with his IQ. Not at first anyway."

"So your husband wasn't very good at relationships at first?"

"I don't know that I would say that exactly. But I think some men struggle. But they can learn. They can figure it out. I do think that sometimes women want men to feel things that men just don't feel. And we think that means they don't love us if they don't feel the way we do. But that's not the way it works. They just don't feel the way we do. They feel differently, or maybe the way they feel love is more intellectual and less emotional."

"Okay. So you're saying my husband probably isn't ever going to put his arm around me and comfort me."

"I think what I'm saying is, you don't think you want to have to tell him that that's what he needs to do, but I'd be willing to bet that if you said to your husband, 'I'm sad that my mom died. I would like you to take an hour off work and sit here beside me with your arm around me, and just sit. Don't talk, just hold me, and be here for me,' he'd do it."

Lauren bit her lip. She wasn't completely sure her husband would actually take an hour off work to do that, but...he was here in Raspberry Ridge, so he'd taken more than an hour. Could she ask him to sit beside her and put his arm around her and comfort her? It just didn't feel the same.

"If I have to tell him what to do, he didn't think of it himself, and therefore that makes it meaningless."

"All right. So, if he doesn't think of it himself, and you don't want to tell him, but you know he'd do it if you asked, why are you upset that he didn't think of it? Does he get upset when you don't think of things that he thinks of? Like the security system? He thought of it, you didn't, was he upset with you?"

"I think he was annoyed, but...no. He's not going to be mad at me tomorrow over that."

"All right. I could be totally off base. But I think your husband loves you, I think he cares about you, and I think you are important to him. He's here, wanting you to come back. He's worrying about you because of the security system. He probably fixes things around the house that maybe you didn't notice."

"I noticed. I didn't always thank him."

"And I don't think he took that to mean you didn't care about him. That was just his way of saying he loved you. You have a different way of saying you love him. I think...if you're going to get what you feel like you need, you're going to have to tell him, 'sometimes I just need you to come over and put your arm around me.' And maybe...if he's as smart as what you say he is, he can start thinking about those times that perhaps you need him. Because you're probably right. He probably doesn't spend a whole lot of time thinking about you or your relationship with him, since he feels like it's okay. He has other things he needs to figure out."

"Yeah. Work things. I guess if he were thinking about silly, inconsequential things, it would bother me more."

She still wasn't sure she completely understood. But she had a better idea of something that she could work on. Although, that was assuming that he still wanted her back. Then there was the question of whether she was going to leave the bakery and go back to Cincinnati. She really didn't want to do that.

"Well, I didn't mean to imply that any of this was all your fault. But I do think that sometimes when couples are having issues, it's hard to see the other person's side. Probably he has more to work on than you do, but I think a relationship can always benefit from both sides working on things."

"That's wise. I guess I just wanted to make him the bad guy and me the good guy, and that absolved me from any kind of responsibility, and I was free to do what I wanted to do."

Except, she really wasn't free. There was no biblical rationale for her to leave.

"Thanks for the bread. I'll let you get back to whatever it was that you were doing. But I really enjoyed talking to you. It's a nice break from my regular life. I spend a lot of time with kids, and adult conversation is something I cherish right now."

"Thanks. And don't let me forget about Bible study." She paused, and then she said, "Would it be possible to have Bible study here? I could make something good to eat. And we'd have something to eat while we studied."

"Everybody usually brings something, and I would hate to have you providing something all the time, but I'm sure that if we put it to a vote with the group, everybody would prefer to come here. I couldn't allow you to do that without being compensated though."

"Maybe you could be on rotation. I was just thinking that I'll probably want to open early, and I probably won't be able to make Bible study unless I missed that first big rush."

"I can talk to everyone. But I bet everyone would be willing to do Bible study earlier or later. Some of us go to work, so we have to work around that."

"All right. I'm not open yet, so I'll show up tomorrow. And bring something."

"All right. I look forward to seeing you again. It's uncommon to find someone who is willing to look at themselves and what they might be doing wrong and to even go further than that and ask someone else what they think. You're definitely a humble person."

Lauren wasn't quite sure whether she agreed with that or not, but she said thank you, and then to her surprise, Skyler came to the break in the counter and started to walk through. She met her, and Skyler gave her a hug.

"I'll be praying for you and your husband. I... I really would like to see your marriage restored and flourishing."

"Thanks. I appreciate that."

She supposed that that was what she should have done to begin with, prayed for her marriage and tried to figure out what she could do to make it better rather than just leaving. Although, leaving had seemed like her only choice at the time. How interesting how other people could open her eyes to possibilities that she didn't even know could be there.

She went to the door and unlocked it for Skyler to leave, and watched as she walked away. She really wanted her husband to change. She didn't want to be the one that had to. But she could see, if she were being honest, places where she could change and be better. And that everything might not be all his fault. It wasn't really fair of her to try to blame him for everything.

It was good that Skyler had opened her eyes today. Now, she just wasn't sure what she was going to do about it.

Thirteen

Cannon stayed in the healing garden until the sun started to go down.

He hadn't eaten anything since the bread his wife had offered him earlier, but he honestly wasn't that hungry.

He supposed it was time for him to get up and find a place to stay for the night. Probably his truck. He could drive to a hotel somewhere, although he'd have to look on his phone to figure out where the closest one was. And he really didn't want to leave his wife. It made him uncomfortable that she was there with no security protection. She had said she wasn't even sure she'd locked the door. That bothered him.

Thinking of that, he pulled up his foreman's contact on his phone and gave him a call. There had been several messages from him, which Cannon had answered as succinctly as possible. Otherwise, he hadn't had any updates on his business for two days.

"George speaking," George answered.

"Hey there. Everything going okay?"

"Yeah. We had a few hiccups, but everything is going fine."

"Good," he said. Normally he would panic over the idea that there had been hiccups and want to know all about them, including what they were and how George had handled them, but right now, that was not at the top of his list of worries. "I need to order a security system, and…" He went on to talk about the kind he wanted and the other specs. He hadn't scoped out the entire house, and he couldn't secure it quite the way he wanted to, but he could do something at least to make sure that if someone came in the windows or doors downstairs, his wife would be woken up and the police called immediately. He had no idea how long it would take the police to come to this godforsaken place, but he was guessing it would probably be a while.

"All right. I can probably have that here in a week."

"No. I need it in Raspberry Ridge, tomorrow."

"Tomorrow?" George said, obviously shocked that he would make such a demand.

"Yes. I need it tomorrow." He knew it could be done. It just would cost. Which was pretty much the way anything was. He could make it happen, but he would have to pay for it. And it would just depend on how much he wanted to pay.

"Boss. That's going to be pricey."

"I know. I want it here tomorrow. Get it ordered, and get it overnighted. If you can't get it overnighted, I want you to personally deliver it."

"All right, boss. If I do this, it means the Crutchfield job is going to be going over budget and time."

"If that has to go over budget and time, that's fine. I want that security system here tomorrow."

"All right, boss. If you say so."

George still wasn't really on board with it and didn't understand why a small system, relative to what they usually put in, would take such precedence, especially over a job like Crutchfield, which was a six-figure job.

"I do. Thanks, George."

He hung up, feeling a little bit better. He wished he would have ordered it earlier that day. He might have been able to get George to bring it out and have it here this evening yet. That way, his wife would be safe tonight, and he would sleep a lot better. Maybe even go to a hotel. But for today, tonight, he was going to be sleeping in front of his wife's store. And he'd be sleeping with one eye open.

He opened the gate and walked out of the healing garden.

He had been so far in his head that he hadn't realized there was someone walking up from what appeared to be the path that went down to the beach, although he wasn't sure. He seemed to vaguely remember Lauren saying something about it when they had visited before, but they'd never been on it themselves.

It was her neighbor, the man that she'd been laughing with when Cannon had walked in the store earlier today.

He jerked his head at the man, not wanting to talk. But the guy stopped. What was his name? Matteo? Cannon wasn't sure, but he didn't want to have anything to do with him. He wasn't sure where the man fit in with his wife, but wherever it was, Cannon wanted to root him out.

"Hey, man." Matteo stopped. He was sweaty, had been jogging, and was slightly out of breath. He put his hands on his hips and walked in place a little, like he didn't want to completely stop and have his muscles get cold.

Cannon respected the self-control and self-discipline it took to have that kind of work ethic to be in that good of shape, but it was hard for him to admit that right now, because...he was jealous of the rapport this man obviously had with his wife.

"I just want to make sure you knew that your wife and I are friends, but I saw the ring on her finger the first time we talked, and it's not been anything more than that. She has definitely kept a straight arm on me, and I don't mess around like that anyway."

"Good to know," Cannon said, not really interested in becoming buddies with this guy. They couldn't have less in common from what he could see.

"She mentioned that you owned a business."

"I do."

"I was wondering if you would give me some advice. I retired recently from the military and civilian criminal investigative work, and I kind of want to chill here in town. But I'm not independently wealthy, and the shop that I inherited from my uncle, which used to be an electronics shop, and I'm turning into a bookshop, is going to need to pay for my food and other necessities." He kicked his legs out and stretched from side to side before he continued. "I was wondering if you had any advice for me. Your wife seemed to indicate that your business was highly successful."

"I built it from the ground up," Cannon said, responding to the man's sincere compliment. He didn't believe it was flattery. And he also believed that the guy probably didn't know squat about business and truly was interested in learning.

"Impressive," the dude said. He gave a half smile. "I'm pretty disciplined, but I don't know anything about business. If it takes hard work, I can do it. But... Knowing exactly how to advertise and market my stuff... I have no clue."

"Are you interested in reading?" Cannon had to ask. The guy didn't look like he'd cracked a book in his life, unless it was a police procedural or a military intelligence manual.

"I read some true crime, thrillers, psychological thrillers. That's about everything."

"I see. Well, my first recommendation would be for you to open a business that suited your interests."

"I like to read. I've probably read ten books over the last ten years."

Cannon managed not to laugh. The dude must have seen the twinkle in his eye though, because he stopped fidgeting for just a moment and said, "That's not enough, is it?"

"In my opinion, I would say no. After all, if you're going to sell books, you've got to know books."

"I have to admit, I've gotten some romance books that have come in the mail, and I've been tempted to tear the covers off them. Wow." He ran a hand through his hair, and Cannon found himself liking the guy despite himself.

"I wouldn't rip the covers off. The cover is the first thing that people see, and I know that the old adage is you can't judge a book by its cover, but I would guess that that's what sells the book. Or at least draws the reader's interest to that particular book."

"That must be why bookstores have displays that show the covers. I kind of thought the spine would be the most important."

"Only true readers go browse. They have to look at spines. Even libraries have displays where you see the cover. They might even have signs that draw your attention to the display before your attention is drawn to the cover. It's all about positioning it and marketing it correctly."

"This sounds a little more complicated than what I was thinking. I thought I'd open a bookstore, because it just didn't seem like a whole lot of work, and I figured that I could work out in the back while people browsed. I'd have the cash register nearby, and I'd check them out and keep doing what I needed to. I don't want to not stay in shape, you know?"

Cannon nodded. He already knew the guy that well. He probably spent a couple of hours in the gym every day. Or a couple of hours running along the lake. It probably wouldn't hurt Cannon to get a little better shape. Maybe, after he was done talking about running a bookstore, he could see if Matteo would give him a little bit of advice on how he should start getting back into shape. Maybe that was part of Lauren's problem, although she'd never mentioned it. Not even once.

"I suppose that would work. I think you're right. People who want to read books aren't really going to need you to take their hand and lead them around the store. You're probably not going to have a lot of customer service issues either."

"No. I'll probably buy back books that were bought in my store, but for less, you know? I'd sell them for some amount and then buy them back for a tenth of that."

"Yeah. That sounds good."

"Where can I learn how to sell books?"

Cannon was quiet for a bit. Really, Matteo should ditch the whole book idea, although he didn't know how much money Matteo already had invested. But he'd be better off getting into something he knew a little bit about. But how would one combine police procedure and investigations into a career in a small-town shop in Raspberry Ridge?

"Raspberry Ridge really isn't big enough to sustain a lot of shops, although... The potential for tourism is there. But someone would have to open up a hotel or inn or something."

"Actually, I heard the inn up on the hill right behind Raspberry Ridge is going up for sale. If that's true, and someone buys it, we might get some tourism, and that's what it's going to take."

"Well. I hadn't heard that." Of course not, since he wasn't from Raspberry Ridge, and the only person he really wanted to talk to here was estranged from him.

"So... Maybe a bookstore would work after all?"

"How much do you have invested in the bookstore so far?"

"I inherited the store from my uncle, and..." He named a figure that he'd invested in a bunch of used books he'd bought online from a store that was going out of business.

It was high three figures, but it didn't sound like a whole lot to Cannon.

"How much do you have to invest in your business?"

"Well, when I retired, I looked into it, and it said that you should have at least ten grand set back. So I do, but... That's my savings too, so if I don't have to spend it all, I don't want to."

Suddenly, Cannon knew exactly what Matteo should do.

"If I were you, I'd sell those books, buy exercise equipment, and open a gym."

As soon as he said that, Matteo's eyes lit up. "That's brilliant."

"Sure. You wouldn't have to be there all the time. You could make it so that members get some kind of card that opens the door, and the door logs it. I actually can help you find a system that will work for that and install it for you."

"A system... Like a security system?"

"Sure. Where the door's locked all the time, but members use their cards. That way you can have—they can have availability 24/7 to the gym. You won't have to be there all the time. You could actually have hours where you're open, for people who want to pay for a one-time deal. That would be like your tourist people. So you'd have it open from like five in the morning until 10 or something like that. And then maybe open in the evening again, whatever the peak hours are for people to exercise." He really didn't know a whole lot about it, other than he had installed four or five security systems for gyms, so he knew that that was a thing, where they had morning hours and evening hours, which were apparently peak hours for exercisers. Although, when he'd had to do some maintenance to one of the systems, he'd been surprised at the people that were there in the middle of the night. Probably that's when the introverts came out.

"It seems like you know a lot about this. Is that what your business is?"

"No. I work in security systems. So I wasn't trying to sell you a system, I was just telling you what I'd learned from putting systems in three or four gyms back in Cincinnati."

"I see."

Matteo actually seemed interested, like he was considering this. Cannon felt bad for thinking that he probably had no intelligence. He'd thought some really unkind things about him, but he turned out to be not such a bad guy after all. It was his jealousy over his wife that had been talking. Still, just because he was jealous, just because he didn't like seeing his wife be all chummy with some guy when she couldn't manage to say two nice words to Cannon, didn't mean that he wasn't supposed to act like a Christian anyway.

He felt like he should apologize, but the dude didn't know his thoughts. Instead, he asked forgiveness from the Lord for the lack of kindness and empathy that he'd had in his thoughts when he first met Matteo.

"I'll have to look, but I bet I can purchase all the gym equipment I need for less than five grand. I probably don't need a whole lot to begin with."

"No. If the tourist trade really picks up here, you might want to expand, but to start out with, you wouldn't need a whole lot." He paused and then lifted a shoulder. "I still don't know whether you'd actually make a profit in a town this size, but maybe there are more people living here than what I thought. Still, you might be able to find stats online, something like if there were ten thousand people living in a town, what percentage of those people have membership at the local gym? That ought to give you an idea of how much money you can make a month. And figure out whether it's going to be enough to provide for your basic necessities."

"Holy cow. That's...well. Yeah. If I knew how many people lived in Raspberry Ridge—"

"That information should be available online. It might not be completely up-to-date, but it should give you a rough ballpark."

"And then I figure out how many of those people are likely to have a gym membership—"

"You should to be able to find that out online by using percentages. I'm sure that information's somewhere."

"Then yeah. I can figure out how much I should potentially be able to make, to start with. That doesn't include the tourists who walk in for a day or two of exercising."

"I would charge a bit more for them. Like if a monthly membership fee is a hundred bucks or a hundred fifty bucks, I don't know, because I don't belong to a gym."

"That's pretty baseline. One fifty to two hundred in the city, one twenty to one fifty out here."

"Then you'd want to charge say fifty bucks for a two- or three-day pass. If they're here for a week, then maybe seventy dollars per week. They'd feel like they're getting a bargain if they buy the week, but most people go on a week vacation, right? So you actually make more on a two-week vacation, and they would be slightly better off buying the monthly membership for a hundred twenty bucks."

"Well. That's smart."

"Yeah. There's lots of little things you can do—marketing tricks and that type of thing that I picked up. I can talk to you about it more if you need to."

"Yeah. Thanks. I probably ought to get going. But I appreciate your help."

"Sure."

Matteo walked quickly away, and Cannon was bummed that he wasn't hanging out longer in Raspberry Ridge, because if he were, he could pick Matteo's brain on what he should do to start getting in shape. Maybe he could still do that and just take the information back to Cincinnati with him and get started back there. He didn't really relish the idea of being miserable, because that's what he equated exercise with, but...he wasn't getting any younger, and if that was the kind of man that Lauren was attracted to, it probably wouldn't hurt for him to bulk up a bit on his physique.

Fourteen

Lauren stood at the window in her small living room overlooking the street of Raspberry Ridge. The sun had gone down, and she was ready to go take a shower and read for a bit before bed, but she didn't want to go back to her bedroom until her husband's truck left. He was sitting in it, just sitting in front of her store.

Cannon wasn't going to stay there all night, was he?

But she'd been waiting for more than forty-five minutes for him to leave, and he hadn't.

As far as she knew, his truck hadn't moved all day. That meant that the bread that she'd given him that morning was the only thing that he had eaten all day.

She paced from the window to the kitchen counter and back. Her hands holding her stomach, her head lifted toward the ceiling, like there were answers there. She did not want to feel responsible for him, and she did not want to feel guilty that he was probably down there hungry and uncomfortable.

Was he expecting her to invite him in?

She supposed she could. She had a couch, and he could sleep there, but that was pushing the boundaries of what she wanted to establish.

After all, she didn't want him to think that he could just move in. Even if he was her husband.

Why not?

Like she had just thought, he was her husband. He had every right to live here if he wanted to. That's the way marriages worked. People lived together. They didn't drive off to a different state and start a business and just leave without saying anything. The way she had done.

She was not going to invite him in, but she'd go down and find out what he was planning, and maybe make a suggestion as to where he could stay tonight. There was a nice inn in Blueberry Beach and another one in Strawberry Sands. Neither one of those were more than half an hour away.

With that determined, she grabbed a sweatshirt from the chair, knowing that it probably had grown cool since the sun went down, despite the fact that it was summer, and hurried out of her apartment and down the steps, through the bakery, and carefully unlocked the front door.

She made sure it was unlocked before she stepped out and closed it behind her. She did not want to get locked out, even though now she was slightly less afraid because her husband was here. She knew if she accidentally locked herself out, he could get her back in. And he wouldn't abandon her until she was taken care of.

Did that show that he loved her? She was looking for comfort and attention, and he was giving her protection and little acts of service.

Had they really just miscommunicated that badly?

She knocked on his window, and he startled, although from what she could tell, he was just sitting in his seat with his hands over his stomach, his seat stretched out as far back as it would go from the pedals.

He tried to open the window, but he needed to turn the truck on first.

"Sorry. Didn't see you there. What do you need?"

"What are you doing?"

He paused, looked around, his face confused. She didn't think he was putting on a show. Theater really wasn't his thing. He wasn't very good at acting.

"I'm going to sleep in my truck in front of your apartment. You don't have a security system on that thing, and it's my job to make sure that nothing happens to you."

That's really how he saw it? It was his job to make sure that nothing happened to her?

That actually made her feel safe and protected. She liked that feeling. And she would have missed it if she hadn't talked to Skyler earlier that day and had Skyler point out to her that maybe he was saying "I love you" in a way that she didn't understand or appreciate.

"Did you eat anything?"

"I had that bread you gave me earlier."

"You're hungry." She didn't have to ask. She knew it. He ate like clockwork during the day. Not that he wouldn't skip a meal for a job or in order to not have to quit early, but she knew he was hungry.

"Yeah. But in case you haven't noticed, there are no fast-food restaurants here, and...no restaurants of any kind."

"I've got leftover spaghetti. I don't have anything fancy, I just made spaghetti to go with my cheese bread and added some garlic and butter to it."

"That sounds good, actually."

Spaghetti wasn't his favorite. And if she did serve spaghetti, she always served meatballs or something with it, because he wanted some kind of protein with his meal.

She didn't have that today, but he didn't complain.

Instead, he put his window back up, turned the truck off, and got out.

"I just feel bad that you haven't eaten. That's all," she said, wanting to say that he wasn't welcome to stay overnight but...not quite being able to bring herself to say that, because he was her husband after all.

He didn't say anything but just followed her to the door, where he opened it and held it for her while she walked in.

He closed it and locked it behind him.

She noticed but didn't say anything.

"I need to heat it up," she said, walking behind the counter to where she had stored the bread. She got a skillet and some butter out and then went to the refrigerator and got the spaghetti. She'd already done the dishes from earlier when she had eaten.

He sat down at the counter and didn't comment while she moved around, eventually going to the refrigerator and coming back with the spaghetti.

"It's awfully nice of you to do this. I wasn't sitting out there so you would see me. I truly was sitting out there to make sure that no one got in."

"You know there's a back door, right?" she asked, smiling a bit. Because he could hardly be in two places at once.

"I know. Still, I was doing what I could."

"I appreciate it. Thank you. That was kind of you." She wasn't sure "kind" was the right word, but it was the word that came to her, and it seemed to fit okay.

"It's kind of you to get some food out and warm it up for me."

She nodded and thought about that for a moment. He was protecting her, he was going to spend all night uncomfortable in his truck, because he wasn't comfortable with the security system she had for her bakery. She, on the other hand, was just going to spend ten minutes heating up food for him. It didn't really feel like a fair trade.

"I was thinking about what you said earlier," she finally started, thinking that maybe she could say something to fill the silence. And she didn't know what was going to happen, but he was here, and he obviously wanted her back, and she might as well try to put into practice what Skyler had said.

"And?" he asked, and she heard a note of eagerness in his voice. She felt bad, because she kind of thought that he was hoping that she would say that she had decided to go home.

"And I just wanted to say that the reason I left is because I felt lonely and alone. I wanted you to comfort me after my mom died. You know, sit beside me and put your arm around me and just hold me."

"I did that." He sounded offended.

"Once, for ten minutes."

"You wanted more?" He sounded truly surprised and baffled.

"Yeah. Hours' worth. I wanted you to take off work and come home and hold me. I wanted to spend time with you after her death."

"Every time I looked at you after that, you started crying. I just thought you didn't want me around."

"I wanted to be able to cry. I wanted to be able to grieve, and I wanted you with me."

"You didn't say that."

"I know. I'm saying it now," she said, trying not to get angry. He wasn't attacking her, he was just pointing out reasons why he didn't do what she'd wanted him to do, and of course he was going to be a little defensive, because she basically was telling him he didn't do a good job of being a husband.

"Oh," he said, and he was quiet.

She flipped the cheese bread in the skillet, spread some butter over the top of it, and sprinkled some garlic powder on that.

She continued to stir the spaghetti.

Then, she left it cooking on the stove while she got a plate out, and a cup and fork while she was at it.

She filled the cup up with cold tap water and set it in front of him.

"Thanks," he said, and he picked it up and drained it.

She smiled a little, because it didn't surprise her that he was thirsty, and he never drank anything except for water in the evening. She took his cup and filled it up again. That time, he didn't touch it.

By then, the garlic bread and the spaghetti were done, and she scooped them out on the plate and set it in front of him.

"I'm sorry I didn't hold you and take off work like you wanted me to."

"I guess that's probably my biggest thing. In your life, work is number one. Wife is...more down at the bottom."

"That's not true at all."

She lifted a brow and then turned back to wipe down the stove and put the spaghetti away.

When she had returned to stand in front of him, he'd prayed silently for his food and started eating.

"It may not feel that way to you. But that's the way it felt to me." She took a breath. "My feelings are valid, even if they maybe don't take into account everything that you're doing. After all, if I give you a present of the biggest diamond in the world, you're not going to be very excited about it, unless you think you can sell it and get money out of it. Because diamonds don't mean anything to you, am I right?"

"Yeah," he said with a forkful of spaghetti halfway to his mouth.

"All right. So if you give me a gift of making your business super successful so that it makes seven figures a year and wins a bunch of prestigious awards, that's for you, not for me. Because it's not what I want."

"You don't want the security of a successful business? You're not proud of your husband for building something like that out of nothing?"

"Of course I want security, and of course I'm proud of you, but when it requires that you spend every waking minute focused on your business, and you have no waking minutes left to talk to me, or to notice that I'm grieving, or to understand that our miscarriage was more than just a couple of cells leaving my body, and that it devastated me, and that I wanted to talk about adoption and you didn't want to have anything to do with it, then it's a problem."

She'd ranted a bit, and she deliberately closed her mouth and took a calming breath.

"I don't know if I understand the appeal of children. They're messy, demanding, and you're miserable while you have them. I just saw my sister and her husband, and they looked exhausted, like they hadn't slept since the babies were born, and I know my sister was up all night, she got maybe five minutes of sleep, if that."

"Those are some of the sacrifices that you make for children. I'm willing to make those, I want to make those. Just because you're inconvenienced doesn't mean it's not worth it."

He seemed to think about that, but she knew he didn't agree.

"When you have a problem with your business that you have to spend a lot of time and money solving, you don't think 'all this is inconvenient, why did I ever start this business?'"

"Sometimes I do," he said around a mouthful of spaghetti.

Apparently he wasn't trying to impress her enough that he would actually wait until his mouth was empty before he talked. But she didn't mind. That was what happened when people were comfortable with each other, right? She'd liked that part of marriage. She liked that comfortableness, that total lack of self-consciousness when he was around. She could be herself, and he loved her anyway. Or at least, he was supposed to. That was the way she thought of him too. He could be comfortable with her, and she would love him anyway. Could be totally himself, not put on any kind of civilized trappings at all, and she would love him anyway. Just him. Not the persona that he showed to the rest of the world.

"Okay, so parents probably think, 'what was I thinking,' when they have children. But you don't for one second think it would be a good idea to sell your business, right?"

"Yeah. I understand what you're saying. The inconveniences are annoying at times, but the overall joy I get out of it makes it more than worthwhile." He got joy out of his business. That seemed to be a revelation, and at the same time, it hurt.

"Do you get joy out of your marriage?" she asked.

He blinked, surprised, and this time, he kept his mouth closed, chewing thoughtfully.

"I don't know that I've ever thought of it that way before, but yeah. Marriage might be a bit of an inconvenience at times..." He looked around ironically, and she understood what he was trying to say. It was a huge inconvenience for him to be in Raspberry Ridge right now rather than running his business where he felt he belonged. "But it's more than worth it. You're more than worth it."

"I guess I just didn't feel like that was the way you truly feel."

"That's a lot of feelings. Could you put it into words that I understand?" He was kind of kidding, she was sure, but that went back to what Skyler was saying. The man was smart, so smart it was almost sinful, and yet...he couldn't figure the simplest of relationship ideas out.

"I think it goes back to the diamond. If I give you a diamond that you need a wheelbarrow in order to haul around, you're not going to appreciate it. Because it's not what you want. You're not going to look at that and go, 'boy, my wife really loves me.' You're going to look at that and be like, 'boy, what did I do to tick her off that she gave me this big old rock to haul around?'"

"I gave you rocks to haul around?"

"You were giving me...things that made you feel like you loved me, and you didn't care how it made me feel. Or you expected me to feel a certain way and didn't bother to take time to check and see if what you did actually made me feel the way you thought it would."

She got too many feelings in there again, and she lost him. She could see it in his eyes.

"So... You just made me supper. I assume you did that because you love me. I am sitting out in my truck in front of your house to make sure that no one breaks in. Are you not assuming that I'm doing that because I love you?"

"Yes. I'm assuming that you love me. But if I had dumped a bunch of rocks on your plate and set it in front of you, you wouldn't have appreciated it, right?"

"Yeah," he said slowly, nodding once, but obviously the light was not dawning.

"All right. But if I put actual food that you like on your plate, you're going to see that as a good thing from me, right?"

"Yeah."

"All right. So I need you to sit with me, to take off work, to show me that I'm more important than your job and your business when I'm sad, and I want my husband to put his arm around me and tell me that it's going to be okay. That's how I feel loved, not when you sit in front of my store protecting me from something that's not there."

"We already went through this. It's when you let your guard down—"

"I know. But I don't see a threat, so for you to do that, you're actually making yourself feel good. You're not really making me feel good."

Fifteen

His mouth opened, but she could see him rolling it around in his head. Could see him realizing that what he was doing was actually gratifying himself, and yes, he was showing love, but he was showing it in a way that made himself feel good.

"So, I think I get it. I'm saying 'I love you,' and you're hearing… nothing?" he said, sounding uncertain and then puttering off at the end. Like he wasn't sure.

"Yeah. I can see that you're doing it because you love me, but it doesn't mean as much to me as if you would have come home from my mother's funeral and said, 'I've taken a two-week vacation, would you like to go somewhere, or would you like to just sit here on the couch together?'"

"You really wanted me around for two weeks after your mother died? I felt like you got irritated if I spent more than five minutes in your presence."

"I was irritated. Sad. Just little things brought memories back, making me cry. I wasn't crying because of you. I was crying because I felt okay and comfortable in front of you."

"I wondered about that, because you couldn't shed a tear at the funeral. It was weird that you didn't cry at all, and then we got home and were alone together and you couldn't stop. It kinda made me feel like it was my fault that you were crying."

"I'm sorry. I didn't mean to make you feel like anything was your fault."

She did understand how he might have gotten confused. And maybe if she had told him why she was crying, that would have alleviated some of his confusion.

"If you had known that I wanted you to stay, I'm pretty sure you would have stayed. But what I really wanted was for you to know that I wanted you to stay without me telling you that I wanted you to stay."

"That is messed up," he said, and despite the seriousness, to her anyway, of the subject matter, she laughed.

"It's not that hard. I feel like it says that you care about me if you know what I want without me having to tell you."

He took a deep breath then and blew it out.

She waited for a bit, and then she said, "When you see a problem at work, the problem doesn't come up to you and say, 'hey, this is what the problem is, and this is what you need to do to solve it.' No, you have to think about that problem, you have to figure it out, you have to try something and maybe that doesn't work, so then you try something else, and then you finally figure out a solution, and you're pretty pleased and proud of yourself. It was fun for you, you were engaged, you cared about it, you showed that it was important to you by sitting there and figuring it out until it was solved."

"Yeah," he said slowly, cautiously, maybe because he heard the anger in her voice. She tried to modulate it.

"But when you see me, you see me crying, you're like 'oh, I gotta get away from that, I gotta go to work and get away,' and you don't think 'hey, I need to figure out what's wrong. I need to figure out what I need to do.' You don't spend one extra second thinking about anything that you could do for me. You just go bury your head in things you enjoy and expect me to take care of myself."

"Well, you are an adult," he started.

"And you're my husband. What's the point in having a husband if I don't have a partner? Someone who cares about me? Someone who sees a problem, and instead of trying to figure out what he can do to alleviate the situation, he just flees. Wouldn't I be better off here in Raspberry Ridge, opening my mother's bakery and taking care of myself, since I'm an adult?"

There. That was really what she wanted to say. There was no point in her staying married, because he didn't care. That's what she saw.

He blinked. And then nodded. And then, she knew he was thinking about what she'd said, because he said, "Is it cheating if I ask someone for help?"

She wanted to cry. And then she remembered sitting on the porch with Skyler, who'd helped her open her eyes.

"Kind of. After all, if you were figuring out a problem at work, you'd spend a little bit of time on it, but you might call someone and say, 'hey, have you ever run into this before,' and they'd give you a hand. So... I guess that's still putting some effort into it. Okay. So asking for help is a little bit cheating, but okay." She huffed out a laugh despite herself and then shook her head. "This is not funny."

"You're the one that's laughing," he said, shrugging his shoulders and putting his hands up like he was innocent.

"You're the one that made a joke."

"You're the one who said you couldn't decide whether you preferred intelligence or a sense of humor, and you were glad I came with both."

"That was then. Not in the middle of a serious discussion. I want your intelligence, and your sense of humor can come... Actually, you're right. A sense of humor and intelligence are equally important, and when you have intelligence along with a sense of humor, sometimes it makes a sense of humor even better." She really did like his sense of humor. She kind of forgot about it. She hadn't been on the receiving end of it for quite a while.

"I was afraid to make jokes after your mother died. I...saw you crying and thought you wouldn't appreciate my jokes."

"I think I needed your jokes more than ever then. And when have I ever gotten seriously mad at you for making me laugh? Even if it was a bad time?"

"True."

"I'm sad about the miscarriages too." She said it, then looked at him.

He looked down. "I feel really helpless about that. I can't fix that.

Just like I couldn't fix your mother dying. I want to fix things. I don't want to sit around and think about them. And... I understand that you want me to sit and hold you, but do you understand that the same way that me not holding you makes you sad, me having to sit and do nothing is hard for me? Right?"

"Sometimes I do hard things for you. Don't you remember that time you had me dangling off the top of the ladder, right beside those live electrical wires, when you were trying to get that first big security system in, before you had any kind of decent help or any knowledge about little tricks you can do to avoid that stuff?"

"I do remember that. Sometimes I wake up in the middle of the night in a cold sweat, because I can see you falling backward into those wires, and I think, 'what in the world was I thinking?'"

"That's funny. I've never lost any sleep over it at all, but you know, there were a few things I did that I didn't enjoy." That would be at the top of the list.

"All right. I suppose if you can climb to the top of ladders near live electrical wires, I can sit with you for a while."

"Gee. Thanks. I really feel like you love me now." She didn't even try to keep the sarcasm out of her voice.

But he laughed. He had liked her sense of humor once upon a time too. She wondered if she had completely lost it. Sometimes it felt like it was buried so deep she'd never get to it again.

They stood looking at each other for a bit, and then she looked down at his plate which had been empty for a while.

"If you come by in the morning, I'll be making sticky buns. But there's no dessert tonight."

"I was thinking I probably should start giving up dessert. I thought I might ask Matteo for some advice on getting back in shape."

"What?" she asked, pausing as she reached out for his plate.

"He asked me for some advice on his business venture, and I told him some hard things. He...seemed appreciative."

"Hard things? You were nice to him, right? Please tell me that you were nice to him? Because he is my neighbor."

"Yeah. I just told him straight up my best business advice, and he really seemed to love it, even though it wasn't easy advice."

"You're scaring me, Cannon."

"And I'm wondering why you're so defensive about this dude. He looked to me like he's more than capable of taking care of himself."

"I just want you to be nice to him. There wasn't anything going on between us, and you were already really rude. I just didn't want you to be rude again."

Was he jealous? Was that why he was so rude? Or was he just upset that he thought that she was cheating on him?

That was probably it more than anything else.

"I wasn't rude. I just told him I thought he ought to open a gym rather than a used bookstore."

"You are brilliant," she said, meaning it entirely.

"Go ahead, say it again," he said, grinning a bit.

"You don't need me to tell you that you're brilliant. You already know it."

"I don't feel that way right now. Not with my wife a thousand miles from where she's supposed to be, where I want her. And she's telling me that for a long time I haven't been a very good husband. That definitely doesn't make a man feel brilliant."

"I'm sorry." She didn't mean to make him feel bad. But how else was she supposed to get her point across?

And the answer came, which was basically what Skyler had said earlier, that she should have talked to him about it a long time before this.

"Some of this is my fault. I should have talked to you about it."

"If you would have just told me—"

"That's just it. It's like what we were talking about earlier, when you see a problem in your business. The problem doesn't tell you what you need to do as a solution, you have to figure it out. That means you care enough to take the time to think about it, to see that there is a problem, and to work on fixing it. I wanted you to do that with me. That, to me, would say that you cared enough about me to see that there was a problem and figure out what you needed to do in order to fix it."

"Yeah. I can see that."

She took the plate off and washed it in the sink while he sat there.

She dried it and put it away, along with his fork and glass. And then she scrubbed the skillet.

Finally, when she was done, he was still sitting there. She walked back over in front of him.

"You really don't need to sit in your truck all night guarding the door. I promise, nothing is going to happen."

"That's not a promise you can keep. I'll sit there."

She pressed her lips closed, but she didn't argue anymore, and as much as she wanted to, she did not offer to let him sleep inside. She... wasn't sure quite why. They were getting along fine. They'd hardly ever argued or fought. She just didn't know what he was going to do. Didn't know if he thought that she was worth the effort to try to figure out. That was what she wanted. To be worth his effort.

But he needed to be worth hers. She needed to make the effort to see what he did as showing her that he loved her, and what if he never changed?

What if she was married to a man who would listen to her talk but wasn't interested in changing, and he wasn't going to do what she felt like she needed, although Skyler had had a good point about that too. If she needed it, God had promised to supply it, so if He hadn't supplied it, she must not need it.

Still, would she be able to live with a man who wasn't willing to change?

She hoped she would be. But if Cannon said that he was willing to change, and he wanted her to come back anyway... She'd have to think about that, but she was pretty sure that biblically, she was required to do it.

"Make sure you lock the door after I leave, okay?" Her husband stood at the door, his hand on the knob, looking over his shoulder at her. He wasn't making a request exactly, but he wasn't issuing a command, like he didn't care whether or not she agreed. She appreciated the fact that he was making it clear that he wanted it done but wasn't treating her like she was two.

"Okay," she said. "Good night."

He nodded, one lip pulling back, as he looked down. "Good night." He opened the door and walked out, and she walked over immediately and locked it. Noting that he stood on the other side, watching until she did.

He mouthed "thank you" before he walked to his truck and got back in.

This time, he got in the passenger seat, which she imagined would probably be a little bit more comfortable.

She didn't watch as he settled in, but instead, she pulled the blind down again and slowly walked back through the bakery, to the steps, and ascended into her apartment.

She felt like she was able to get some of the things that had bothered her out in the open. And she had done what Skyler had suggested, which was tell him instead of expecting him to figure it out.

There was still a part of her that really wanted him to work at having her, the same way she worked at trying to figure out what he wanted. Like if they were home, she would never have eaten spaghetti and garlic bread. She would have had meat with it. Because that's what he wanted. She would never not set an alarm or not arm the security code because that's what he wanted, even though she didn't feel like it was necessary. And she would always lock the door, because she knew that's what he wanted.

Maybe she should allow him to work as much as he wanted, because she knew that was what he wanted, but... Shouldn't there be a line drawn when what he wanted directly interfered with putting his wife ahead of everything except for God?

She wasn't quite sure the answer to that, and she was tired of thinking about it for one day.

Sixteen

Cannon awoke with a start, realizing that the noise that had brought him from unconsciousness was tapping on his window. He blinked and squinted, trying to see who it was.

He wished he'd brought a gun.

Then, the person leaned closer, and he could make out his wife's features.

He knew he couldn't wind down the window, so he just grabbed for the latch and opened the door.

She stood, wrapped in a blanket, her hair a little mussed, like she'd been lying down. He didn't even know what time it was. He fumbled around, looking for his phone.

"Would you like to come in and sleep on the couch?" she asked.

He almost laughed. He wished she would have issued that invitation earlier, but she hadn't, and he decided he wasn't going to ask. She had left him, and while he considered what was his was hers and what was hers was his, since they were still married, he wasn't going to push in. He...wanted her to want their marriage of her own free will, not because he forced himself into it.

"I don't want to put you out," he said, assuming she had a bed.

"No. There's a bed in the bedroom, and there's a couch in the living room. You could have it if you want. I...should have offered it earlier. I'm sorry."

That surprised him, and he supposed his brows and open eyes showed her how he felt.

Still, he finally found his phone and looked at it.

Just a little after midnight.

It had only taken her a couple of hours for her guilt to nag her so bad that she would come and offer him the couch.

"That's nice of you. If you truly don't mind, I'll take you up on it."

"Yeah. It would make me feel better if you would. Please."

It was late, and he was still a little groggy from sleep, and she didn't look the greatest either. They could talk in the morning.

So, he followed her silently into the bakery, where he stopped and deliberately turned around and locked the door. Tomorrow, George would have the security system, and he could have it installed in an afternoon. The symbolism wasn't lost on him.

Hopefully tomorrow night, Lauren would feel a lot better. But then, he would have no excuse for sleeping outside. But he wasn't going to leave here without his wife. Not unless she made it clear that she absolutely did not want him and was going to file for divorce.

He didn't like to think that word. Because when he'd vowed, for better or for worse, to be with her for a lifetime, he'd meant it.

And whatever was wrong that was within his realm of ability to save, he was going to save.

He understood that he couldn't make decisions for her, and if she chose to continue on the path that she was on, separation, and eventual divorce, there was only so much he could do to stop her. He wasn't going to stand in her way. That was her choice. But his choice was to stand for his marriage.

He was feeling dramatic though. So, he shut that off and walked silently up the steps behind her, after checking the back door to make sure it was locked. He thought he saw a shadow and stopped to squint.

"I think there's something moving out there," he said.

"It's probably the stray dog I've been feeding. I think it's pregnant."

"You need to be careful with those things. They could have rabies."

"It doesn't have rabies," she said.

She continued up the stairs, and he went to follow her. He wanted to argue. She had no idea whether it had rabies or not, but he supposed her opinion was just as valid and just as reasonable as his. Just because it was a stray dog didn't mean it automatically had rabies.

It was just that rabies was a disease that he didn't want his wife to get. And he wanted to keep her safe, and the safest thing was to not hang out with stray dogs. Whether they were pregnant, or whether they were cute. It made perfect sense to him, but maybe it was one of those things that he saw clearly, and she didn't see at all.

There was a door at the top of the steps, and they walked into the apartment, which, from first glance, was extremely small.

There was a tiny kitchen, a small island that must serve as the kitchen table as well, since he didn't see one of those, and then a living room with a couch and a chair.

There was a small hall with two doors. He assumed one was a bathroom and the other a bedroom. The bedroom couldn't be very big at all, but he'd never been upstairs. In as many times as they'd visited her mom, they'd always chatted downstairs in the bakery. If it was open, they'd chatted around the customers, and if it was closed, they'd had the whole thing to themselves. But he didn't come very often. Maybe that was another thing that she wished were different. If she'd told him that she wanted him to visit more, he would have gone. It wasn't like he didn't enjoy traveling with his wife. He just...had a business to run.

That seemed to be a theme, every time he thought about things, and he wondered... Maybe there was something that he needed to do.

"Here. Let me get you a pillow and a blanket out. I don't think you'll be cold, you usually run hot at night, but if you need more, there's some in the closet in the bathroom."

"All right. Thanks," he said. He watched her as she stood there, her fingers on the couch, looking at the blanket and pillow she'd laid there.

"Thanks for taking care of me," she said, and she didn't raise her eyes to meet his.

"It's my job. It's what I signed up for. I like doing it."

He emphasized that last sentence. And she smiled faintly.

"Good night."

She didn't acknowledge his words. Didn't have any comment about that. Maybe it was for the best, since again, neither one of them were at their best—it being after midnight and they were both extremely tired.

He lay down, stretching the blanket out and figuring that it was the perfect length for him. She knew him very well. Better than he knew her for sure. And yet, his command was to dwell with his wife according to knowledge. She'd made the effort to get to know him, and he hadn't made much effort at all.

He needed to change that. Obviously. Although, it hadn't been obvious to him before this. Before she'd done something so dramatic. He wondered if she would have just said, "Hey, Cannon. I need to talk to you." And then she'd laid it all out. Would he have listened? Would he have changed his mind about anything? Would she have been able to get his attention just like that? Or did he need her to leave in order for him to wake up to what he was doing?

He liked the fact that when they had talked earlier, she didn't blame it all on him. She admitted that maybe she hadn't been perfect either. Honestly, that helped him want to do better, since she wasn't railing against him and telling him how terrible he was.

Maybe leaving was what she had to do in order to get his attention without getting angry and screaming. He'd like to think that he would have been able to have an adult conversation and change things around if she'd just had to talk, but he had a sneaking suspicion that he would have just brushed her off. Maybe not even heard what she had to say. Resented the fact that he had to take time to talk to her when there was work to be done. Maybe he would have thought of her as needy or high maintenance. When he knew she was neither.

He must have drifted off at some point, because he awoke with a start. Was that a car door slamming?

He got up, holding the blanket as he did so and walking over to the window.

He looked down and studied the vehicle for a minute before he realized it was one of his work trucks. George must be here already.

He wasn't expecting that.

He folded the blanket and set it on the couch, and walked softly across the floor, grabbing his boots from the end of the couch where he'd set them last night when he'd taken them off.

"What is it?" His wife's voice stopped him with his hand on the doorknob.

"My foreman, George, is down there."

"I thought that was one of your trucks," she said, pulling her robe tighter against her and furrowing her brows. "What's George doing here?"

Was she going to be mad about this? Normally he didn't hesitate to tell her things, and he didn't worry about her getting mad. But his wife packing up and moving across two states had a tendency to do that to a man.

He figured she was going to find out at some point, so he might as well be honest about it. "I ordered a security system for the shop yesterday. I told him I wanted it here today. He must have gotten it from the warehouse and driven straight through."

"A security system? For here?"

"Yeah. For here. The front door, the back door. It's not going to include the windows upstairs, but it will include the shop windows. I'll feel a lot better once it's in, and I should have it up and running by dusk. Possibly noon if George helps me."

"Oh my goodness. You're serious. You..." She didn't say thanks, and he took that as his opportunity to escape. He didn't even bother putting his boots on until he was downstairs, because he didn't want to get yelled at.

Although, Lauren had never, not once in all their years of marriage, ever yelled at him. Still, he figured what he'd done was going to make her angry. But he wasn't going to undo it. He was going to put a security system in. He was going to take care of his wife. That was the way it was going to be.

Seventeen

"What's going on out there?" Grace asked as the door closed behind her, and she put her nose in the air, sniffing the cinnamon scent appreciatively.

"These are warm, fresh from the oven. You can help yourself right here," Lauren said, pointing to the cinnamon rolls she had taken from the oven just five minutes prior.

"You didn't answer my question," Grace said, coming over and grabbing a cinnamon roll as Lauren put a plate in front of her. "Oh boy, these smell so good. And they're so warm and gooey. You are a danger to my figure." But that didn't stop her from picking up the fork that Lauren had set on the plate and digging into her cinnamon roll.

"Coffee?" Lauren asked.

"Please. And answer my question. What in the world?"

"My husband is putting in a security system." She still couldn't quite believe it. He had had his foreman, the man whom she assumed he had left in charge whenever he left, drive the whole way out here, and now he, the one who usually ran the business, and his foreman George, the one who ran it anytime he absolutely had to be away, like for her mother's funeral, were both out here.

Whatever job they were working on, he had pulled George off it, ordered a security system, and gotten it here in less than twenty-four hours. She had worked in the business enough to know that he was basically pushing off his other jobs and making this job a priority. This job, that didn't pay anything, that wasn't nearly as important as some of the six- and seven-figure jobs he had, and yet...he was acting like it was urgent.

"So... I think he might care about you just a little bit," Grace said slowly.

"I know. I feel so guilty. I—" She came over and stood in front of Grace, lowering her voice and leaning forward just a bit. "I almost made him sleep in his truck last night. I did give him supper, but it was just spaghetti. He doesn't like spaghetti. And if I do have to serve spaghetti, he prefers meat with it. So it was just spaghetti and a piece of garlic bread made out of the cheese bread I made yesterday. Not his favorite. And then, he went to sleep in his truck. And I did all of that, without knowing that he had already ordered the security system and was planning on getting it and putting it in today."

"Oh my goodness. You made your husband sleep in his truck last night?" Grace looked aghast, although she was obviously trying to hide it.

"No. I went out at midnight, because I just felt so stinking guilty. I told him he could come in and sleep on the couch."

"Okay. So you left him out there until midnight, and then you told him he could come in and sleep on the couch?"

"Yes. I am a terrible person, aren't I?" She felt terrible. She had felt justified in what she thought were her perfectly normal grievances, legitimate grievances. And yet, her husband was being so nice, so... protective, and, at the same time, not angry at her, but seeming to try to figure out what he could do to make things better. He wasn't blaming her, and he wasn't railing at her for not just talking to him instead of leaving. Because she kind of felt like that was probably all she needed to do. Just tell him that she wanted to sit down and talk to him, and he would have. He would listen to her. They would have worked it out, and she wouldn't have needed to leave.

"I don't think you're a terrible person. You are hurting. You're hurting because of the miscarriages. You are hurting because of losing your mom. And I don't know that you can necessarily use it as an excuse. But maybe your pain and grief just precluded your ability to think rationally for a little bit."

"It's funny, because I thought I was thinking very rationally. In fact, I would have said that I absolutely had thought it through, looked at all the different angles, and made the best decision. But the more time I spend here, and the more time I spend with him, I think I was wrong. I think I was very, very wrong."

She looked at her husband, who was pointing at something and talking to George. She thought they would have it done by noon at the rate they were going.

"Everybody's entitled to be wrong."

"But I left him! I mean that's not just wrong, that's exceptionally, horribly, stupidly wrong."

"He doesn't look like he's going to hold it against you. In fact, far from holding it against you, it looks to me like he's helping you. Would he be putting in a security system if he was expecting you to move back to Cincinnati?"

That was a rational question she hadn't considered.

"Do you think that he's given up on getting me back?" She hadn't expected him to come after her at all, and now she was surprised at how quickly she had gone from not expecting him to come after her, to expecting him to fight for her, to now being scared to death that he was just going to let her go.

"I highly doubt it. But he's obviously showing how much he cares about you."

"I suppose you're right."

"I hate to eat and run, but I have to go to Bible study. I actually was dropping by to see if you wanted to come."

"I was planning on coming, but I'm not going to leave with my husband here."

"Totally understandable, and I think that's the best decision. I'll stop by later, if I get a little free time."

"All right. Thanks. Good to see you," she said, feeling bad that they'd spent their whole time together talking about her and her problems. She should have been more considerate and asked her friend about herself.

But she supposed when someone was going through something, friends made allowances for them to be extra preoccupied with themselves.

She hoped she did that anyway.

It looked like it was going to be a little while, she thought as she gathered up Grace's dirty plate and fork and her empty coffee cup and washed them.

She dried them and put them away, and then she grabbed the scraps she'd set aside the day before and went to the back door.

She'd set some food out earlier, and it was gone.

The dog must have been getting more used to her, because it stood by the peach grove, its tail slowly going back and forth.

"Are you hungry, honey?" she asked, walking down to the bottom step, setting scraps of food down, and then coming back up and sitting at the top step.

The dog was shaggy and gaunt with its hip bones sticking out and shoulder blades clearly visible along with each of its ribs.

But it had a bit of a distended belly, and that's what made her think it was pregnant.

Hopefully the puppies weren't all born dead. That would be sad. She'd had enough sadness for a while. Surely God wouldn't send her a stray dog, that was pregnant, no less, and then have all the puppies die in her care.

Not that this was really in her care. Maybe she could go get dog food later today. She should have done that when she first saw the dog, rather than grabbing scraps and using those. The dog could use balanced nutrition.

"I'm sorry. Maybe that's why I don't have a baby of my own. I'm not very good at taking care of things. I have a tendency to jump to the wrong conclusions and go running off when I shouldn't."

She didn't really have a tendency to do that. This was the first time in their marriage that she had, but she'd been harboring these resentments for a while now.

As she spoke, the dog continued to stand there wagging its tail.

"Come on, honey. I won't hurt you. And you don't have rabies. You're just really hungry."

Maybe the dog had gotten lost or had accidentally jumped in someone's car that was just driving through.

Maybe someone had realized it was pregnant and dropped it off.

Whatever its story was, it seemed like it had been a long while since it had had someone regularly feeding it.

"Don't be afraid. I'll try to get you more food later. Although, too much at one time will probably make you sick. And that won't help you at all either, will it?"

The dog started coming closer, slowly.

Its eyes were sweet, its head down, its tail still swaying slightly back and forth.

But its whole body was focused on the food on the step. The poor thing was starving.

She wasn't quite sure what kind of dog it was. Probably a mix of a bunch of different breeds, but she thought she saw a little bit of golden retriever in it. That's probably where the long shaggy hair came from. But the white collar around its neck and the white paws... She wasn't sure. She didn't really know of any dogs that looked like that. Those were more like horse markings. At least the white feet.

"Come on, sweetheart. If you eat that, I'll see if I can find something else for you in a bit."

She tried to remember how many eggs she had in the refrigerator. She had been going to offer to cook some for Cannon this morning, so she hadn't even opened the refrigerator to get anything for herself. She thought she had two or three left. Cannon would need at least two and more if she didn't have anything to go along with it. But there was a little bit of bacon in the refrigerator as well. So she could give a whole egg, and maybe two, to the dog.

Still, it would be better to get some dog food.

By that time, the dog had walked almost the whole way over and was now in a crouch, slinking forward, its eyes on the food. Lauren sat as still as she could.

"Lauren!" a voice said at the same time the door opened. The dog spun around and fled away. Lauren turned, her husband standing behind her, anger on his face but also worry and concern. "What are you doing? That dog looks like a mangy old thing that has a million diseases."

"She's pregnant and hungry. She almost came to me. That was the closest she'd ever gotten." She stood, knowing that the dog wasn't going to be coming back anytime soon. She was angry with her husband for scaring it away.

But her anger was tempered by the fact that she knew he was trying to protect her, and with her newfound knowledge, she was assuming that that meant that he was showing that he loved her. Even if he was irritating her rather than making her feel loved.

He took a breath, blowing it out and shoving a hand through his hair. "I'm sorry. I just saw that dog out there, it looked rough, and you were so close to it, and I... I wanted to scare it away. I was worried about you."

"Thanks. I appreciate the fact that you were worried." She didn't appreciate the fact that he had scared the dog away, but there would be another time for the dog to come, and she'd leave the food there.

"I just came in to tell you that we have another hour, and then we're going to be finished. George is going to have to go, but I wanted to know if you wanted to go to a restaurant and eat brunch?"

When was the last time they'd gone out to eat together? Maybe when her mom was sick and they'd had to run an errand and he had gotten home late and she was still up... It was still more than a year ago.

Because he couldn't take off work.

"Sure. I actually wanted to go down to Blueberry Beach and grab a bag of dog food. She needs more balanced nutrition than what I have for her. It probably wouldn't hurt for me to grab some groceries too."

"If groceries mean that you're going to be making more of your delicious baked goods, like your cheese bread yesterday, and your cinnamon rolls today, I am all about groceries." He looked a little sheepish. "I hope those cinnamon rolls on the counter were for anyone to eat, because I just ate two. And George might have had one too."

"Yeah. I actually thought you would prefer eggs, but I didn't want to take you from your work."

"You're right. I would prefer eggs, but those cinnamon rolls will hold me over until we go to eat in an hour, if you're sure that's okay?"

"Yeah. It sounds great."

Did she just agree to go on a date with her husband? Did the date include grocery shopping? She supposed that's how a person knew they were married, when something like grocery shopping constituted a date.

"All right. I... I'm sorry again about the dog, but... I would feel safer if I was around if you're going to try to pet it or anything."

"I won't try to pet it now. I'll come in and tidy up a bit, and get ready to go. I'll make a list of the things I need."

"All right. We'll plan to pull out in an hour, unless something comes up." Her husband stopped as he held his hand on the door, getting ready to open it for her. "Never mind. We'll get ready to go in an hour, no matter what comes up. How's that?"

"If something comes up, it's okay. I... I get it."

"I guess I'm just not very good at this, but I want to try."

"Okay."

She wasn't sure what he was trying or what his plans were. Maybe that was something they could talk about over brunch.

With that, he opened the door, and she walked in ahead of him.

<h1>Eighteen</h1>

Cannon opened the door of his truck, and his wife got in.

He was nervous, as nervous as though this were their first date.

He was tempted to run his sweaty hands down over his jeans, but he at least needed to wait until she got in the truck and then try to unobtrusively do that while he was walking around to get in the driver's seat.

He had been nervous about asking her, and then he'd managed to go and screw everything up by scaring away the dog that she was trying to tame. But that dog looked all mangy and sick, and he really didn't want his wife anywhere near it.

Not because he hated the dog, but because he didn't want anything to happen to his wife.

Why was it so hard for her to understand?

Maybe he just needed to let go. But he couldn't shake the feeling that it was his job to protect her and to see dangers that she didn't.

While she saw things that would help make him more comfortable, like saving the last of the eggs for him or getting him the exact blanket that he needed to be completely comfortable for the night. Anything heavier and he would have been too hot, anything lighter and he would have been too cold. It was perfect. And she knew it.

"I just want to apologize again about the dog," he said after he had gotten in and started the engine and put his seat belt on.

"Don't worry about it. She ended up coming back over and eating the food I left there, so she got what I wanted her to. I just...wanted to tame her down a little bit and have her trusting me so that when it comes time for her to have her babies, I can help her take care of them. There's no shelter outside, and I'm pretty sure she used to be a house dog. She's wearing a collar, but there's no tag on it."

"She might be microchipped."

"Yeah. But I can't tell, and I can't get a hold of her either."

"True."

"I think the closest veterinarian is down in Blueberry Beach. We really could use one here in town."

Maybe this would be a good time for him to ask her what she was planning. And perhaps it would be a good time for him to tell her what he had decided.

"I... I don't want to open a can of worms, because I didn't ask you out to eat with me so that we could fight."

"I don't really think we ever had too much trouble fighting, did we?"

"No. I guess not. I guess I'm just...a little gun-shy right now."

"I'm sorry. That's my fault. I can promise I will try as hard as I can not to get upset about anything."

He figured that was probably the best promise that he could get. But he didn't know what subjects were touchy for her and which ones weren't.

"I wanted to know how long you're planning on staying here?"

She didn't say anything for a bit, twisting her hands in her lap and looking out her window before sighing. "When I left, I was planning on moving here permanently. I wanted to open up my mom's bakery. I've always wanted that, and we talked about it whenever she came to stay with us, remember? She was worried about it."

"Yeah. And you wanted to come out here and keep it open for her, and take care of her too. I thought that was going to be too much for you."

"And you were right. By the time she got really sick, it was all I could do to take care of her, and that was even with some help. There is no way I could have run the bakery too."

He thought that she just said that he was right. She'd given him credit? He glanced over, but she didn't seem to be keeping score or at least wasn't tallying up anything on his side of the scorecard, so he assumed not.

"So you said when you left that's what your plan was. Is that still your plan?"

"I don't know. I honestly didn't think that you cared whether I was there or not, and that was informing what I did."

"I'm sorry you got that impression. And I understand how you got it. I did a lot of thinking last night, and I realize you came to a perfectly logical conclusion. If I don't spend time with you and on you, and I don't think about you and make an effort to...know you, then you have every right in the world to think that I don't care. But just for the record, that's not true."

"I think I figured that out. I... I don't know what to do. I guess maybe I was thinking that we could talk about that today."

"All right. Well, I actually was talking to George today, and he's been interested in buying the company for a while. He's talked about buying other security companies, if I wouldn't sell to him. I just brushed it off, because I have a couple of other guys who will take his place if he does decide to open his own business."

"Okay," she said, looking at him uncertainly.

Of course she had no idea where he was going with that. Because he'd never said a word to her.

"He's going to see if he can get funding, and then if he can, he's going to purchase the company from me."

"You're selling your company?"

"I'm moving here. I didn't know if you'd let me live with you, but if not, there's a house up the street that's for sale. The sign just went up a couple of days ago according to Matteo, and I thought I might see what they wanted for it. The lease is up at our apartment in Cincinnati in two months anyway, so we wouldn't be losing a whole lot. And this is a nice place. A good place to raise children."

There. He'd said it. He realized that after the miscarriages and losing her mom, she felt lonely. She wanted a family. Not just him. She wanted children. Look at her and the stray dog. She was constantly bringing people around her, and...she deserved to have a family. When they got married, they were planning on it.

"Cannon?" she said, like she didn't quite understand what he was saying.

"You can think about it. I haven't made any firm plans. I did want to talk to you about it first. But George is going to do some talking to a couple of different bankers and see what he can come up with."

"Oh my goodness. All right." She seemed stunned. Not necessarily happily stunned, just stunned. He wasn't quite sure what that meant.

They didn't say too much more as he navigated the road toward Blueberry Beach. He needed her to give him a few extra directions, since he wasn't as familiar with these roads as she was.

"If it's okay with you, I thought we could eat before we go grocery shopping. I want to get a few things that need to stay cold."

"That's just fine."

"All right. The diner should be right over here, you can park anywhere along the street."

He found a spot, pulled into it. He shut the engine off and got out, intending to open her door, but she didn't wait for him. How long had it been since he'd opened her door for her?

They hardly ever drove anywhere together. Except church, when he went.

He wanted to take hold of her hand, but he wasn't sure where they stood. She...hadn't said that it was okay for him to be with her. She had left him, after all.

He needed to ask.

The waitress showed them to their seats, and they ordered their drinks and browsed the menus. He waited until after they had both ordered the special and the waitress had delivered their drinks before he folded his hands in front of him and leaned forward.

"I guess I might have been getting the cart before the horse. You...

left me. I'm not sure where that leaves me in our relationship. Do I have the right to hold your hand? Have you changed your mind about leaving me? Where are we? Because... I guess I need you to help me navigate the relationship-type things, because where I can see the danger in the stray dog easily, I don't understand relationships very well."

There. That was as honest as he could be. He wanted to do it right, he just wasn't sure what that was.

"I guess... I guess if you don't want me to leave, I won't. But I think that we should have the talk that we should have had before I left. Instead of leaving, I should have calmly and rationally gone to you and tried to talk to you about this."

"I thought about that. I'm not sure I would have listened. I think that maybe you did the only thing that you could have done to get my attention, and that was to walk out. If you had just talked before you walked, it wouldn't have caught my attention."

She sighed and looked over at the window, which faced an alley.

Then she looked back at him. "No. I know you would have listened. I could have asked you to hold me, and you would have. I could have asked you to take a day off work and do something with me, and you might have groused about it, but you probably would have done it."

"But I wouldn't have liked it. I wouldn't have understood. I wouldn't have seen how desperate you were. How serious you were. How much you felt like I didn't care or love you. I don't recommend doing it again, and I definitely wouldn't recommend it to any other woman, but I think I needed this as a wake-up call."

She nodded, but she didn't smile in triumph, even though he had basically told her that she was right.

Lauren wasn't like that. She was sweet and funny, kind and considerate, not the kind of person who gloated or liked to rub anything in anyone's face. Instead, she'd go out of her way to avoid hurting someone. That was the woman he'd fallen in love with.

That was the woman he was still in love with.

"Okay, just so I know I understand, we're still together, but we're working through some things." He lifted his brows, wondering if he'd got it right.

"That sounds good. Yes. Working through some things."

"So how do you feel about me selling the business?"

"I can't believe it, to be honest."

The waitress came with their meals, chicken and gravy and mashed potatoes and a vegetable on the side, and it smelled delicious. Maybe even homemade.

He waited until the waitress left, and he had said grace, before he picked up his fork and then said, "So you're okay with it?"

"I don't really want you to have to sacrifice everything. I mean, I'd love to be able to run my mom's bakery, but it's kind of impossible for you to have a business in Cincinnati and me to have a bakery in Raspberry Ridge. So we need to figure out who gets what they want and who gives up what they want."

"I guess that seems obvious to me. We've been married for ten years, and in those ten years, I've been building my business the entire time. I've got what I wanted. It's your turn."

He didn't really mean that as a consolation. He meant that sincerely. He'd built his business into a multimillion-dollar thing, and while he highly suspected that George was not going to be able to come up with the money, he thought that it wouldn't be hard to sell to an investment group. The business had been profitable for the last six years, and before that, it had been borderline.

He had jobs lined up to last him the rest of the year, and his reputation was known all around Cincinnati. Maybe he was mistaken, but it felt like he was sitting on, if not a gold mine, a nice little nest egg.

"I don't want you to have to give it up."

"I'm sorry that you ever thought that you were in competition with the business. You're not. You mean far, far more to me than the business ever will. I'm willing to give it up. I want to, actually. I like Raspberry Ridge. Matteo's growing on me too."

"You hated Matteo," she said dryly.

"I don't hate Matteo. I only hated Matteo when my wife was laughing with him and not laughing with me."

She closed her mouth and stared at him for a moment before he looked away. It was the truth. He didn't hate Matteo, he just hated himself for not being able to make his wife laugh and for another man to be able to do it instead.

"Can we think about it?"

"Sure. You can think about it as long as you want to."

"No. I mean us. Together. We can think about it. You might not even be able to sell your business."

"Then I'll just work out the contracts we have, and I'll move to Raspberry Ridge anyway and close up shop."

"Everything you worked for—"

He lifted his shoulders. "It's worthless without you."

Her face softened, and she smiled at him. He felt like that was the exact right thing to say, although he hadn't been saying it to curry favor. He'd been saying it because that's what he meant.

"I need to get back so I can finish that security system, but maybe we can do something tomorrow?"

"Sure. I'd love that. I have plans to meet with Grace and Claire this afternoon anyway," she said, looking across the table at him, and he got the feeling that he was on the right track.

After that, they talked about easy things. Things that weren't going to bog down the conversation and make one or the other of them feel sad and guilty or bad in any way.

The weather, the school system around this area, since she'd gone to it and he didn't. The idea of a small town versus a big city. Pros and cons. She told him he needed to see the beach, and he agreed to go, tomorrow.

He had never been a very big beach person. He hated sand. It got everywhere, like everywhere. He hated that. But she assured him that there was a pebble beach that was very nice, and no sand involved. Although, there was sand on part of the shore farther north.

He could endure sand for Lauren.

He realized why he had married her to begin with. He enjoyed being with her. She was fun, she was funny. She was smart, but not one of the smart people that were so smart that they were boring to talk to. Or uncomfortable to talk to.

She kept him humble. She saw things that he didn't and gave him a wider perspective. He liked what she added to him, and he hoped that he added a little bit to her too.

By the time they were done eating, he was ready to be back to normal. Whatever that was. He supposed that the reason she was hesitant was because their normal was him working all the time and her taking care of her mom, being sad about the miscarriages, and wishing that he was around, when he was oblivious.

They would have to create a whole new normal.

Plus, he figured that she was probably a little bit in disbelief, wondering if he might fall back into his old habits, once he had her securely attached to him again.

He hoped he didn't. He wanted to set up his life so that he didn't.

But he wasn't sure what that would look like.

Nineteen

Grace and Claire were both waiting for her when she hurried into the grove at the healing garden. The date that she'd had with her husband had taken longer than she thought it would. Mostly because they'd lingered over their food, chatting and... At least for her, she enjoyed his company. Remembering all the reasons she'd married him to begin with. He was sweet and funny and attentive. More attentive than he'd been in years.

The problem was, she was worried that this wouldn't last. Maybe this was just something that her leaving him had triggered in him, and once he had her back, he'd go back to neglecting her.

Part of her said that she didn't need to worry about that. Because if he did, obviously he was reasonable. She could talk to him, he could see that he was doing something wrong, and he would fix it. The same way she would if he came to her and said that she was doing something that he would prefer she not do.

Except, she was rebelling about the dog.

That was different though. That wasn't something that was hurting him, that was something that he would prefer she not do, because he was worried about her safety.

Maybe it wasn't different. She was classifying it in her mind differently, but maybe he didn't.

Regardless, she hurried to her friends, who both stood up, and they embraced.

"So nice to be able to meet together. I honestly had been dreading a long, lonely summer all by myself. Especially after Grandma died. But I hadn't expected my kids to come back, Josiah to marry me, and now friends from my past to meet with on a regular basis."

"We should set a regular meeting time," Grace said, looking at Claire.

"Yeah."

"I'd love to do that. I think... I kinda think I might be going to stay."

"And open the bakery?" Grace asked eagerly.

"I think so."

"Does that mean that your husband is going back to Cincinnati without you?" Claire asked, and she looked slightly less enthused.

"No. Actually, I think he's going to sell his business and move here." She didn't want to start a whole bunch of rumors if it turned out to not be true, so she said, "I'd appreciate it if you don't say anything for now. I guess we're still talking about it, but that's what he was saying today when he and I went out to eat. That he wanted to be with me. And that for the last ten years, he'd built his business. Now he wants to sell it and have a little nest egg, I think that's what he called it, and have me run the bakery."

Both of her friends smiled and seemed excited. And then Grace bit her lip.

"But... Would you make enough money to support yourselves?"

"I'm not sure. I mean, Cannon told me today that he had heard around town that someone had bought the inn. Did you guys hear that?"

"I heard a rumor about it," Claire said. "And I hope it's true. But I did a little digging, and I couldn't figure out who it was."

They were silent for a moment. Yolanda's mother had always talked about wanting to buy it, but after Yolanda died, her mother moved away. It was like she couldn't stand the pain.

Which reminded Lauren that maybe this was something she should face too. Because if she had faced her marriage problems, she wouldn't have ended up leaving her husband and causing him a lot of undue stress and worry.

"Can I... Can I talk to you guys about something?"

"Sure," they said together.

They took their seats, with Lauren sitting between Grace and Claire, and both of them kind of slightly tilted toward her.

"They need to put benches that face each other, for people who want to sit and talk."

"I think that they think that most of the people who come here are people who want to sit and think and reflect quietly," Grace said, but she lifted her shoulder. "I certainly don't disagree with you. If people are going to meet here, like us, the seating arrangements are not the best."

"But I love this spot. The shady grove is so beautiful," Lauren said, looking at the trees that sheltered the walkway, protecting it, giving it such a whimsical, beautiful look.

But she was procrastinating. She wanted to talk to them about Yolanda. And that day.

"Is it going to ruin your day if I bring up Yolanda again?" She paused. She felt like she was ready now. Even though not a whole lot of time had passed, just having things...not settled, but better between her husband and her, made her feel like she had the strength to face this.

"No. Grace and I talked about her a while ago, and it really helped me. I...still have times where I don't always like to think about going out on the lake, but I'm more at peace with it than I ever have been."

"Same. It just helped to hear someone else saying that they felt the same things I did."

"I don't know that either one of you will feel what I feel, because most of my feeling is guilt."

"I felt guilt too," Grace admitted.

"Same," Claire said.

"I'm not sure I understand why you guys would, because I'm the one who encouraged her to go. She was going to stay with me. After she found out that I wasn't going to go. I...just didn't feel like it. It wasn't that I had some kind of strange premonition or anything. I just...can't explain it. Normally I was all in for a day on the lake. But I wanted to stay home and just read a book. Maybe—I don't really remember, but maybe the book I was reading was pretty good. Maybe that was it. And also, we had a cat that had just had kittens. I wanted to stay home and keep an eye on them too."

"I think I remember about the kittens." Claire furrowed her brows together. "I kind of forgot about that until you brought it up."

"Yeah. I don't even remember what happened to the kittens. The days afterward were so chaotic, and I felt guilty, because Yolanda came over, and she wanted to sit and play with the kittens. But they were newborns. You couldn't play with them. You could only sit and watch them. And I didn't want her handling them too much."

Lauren bit her lip.

"I guess I was being selfish too. They were new, and I wanted to have them to myself for a bit. Anyway, I wanted to read my book too. So I basically talked her into going. Because she didn't even bring her beach clothes to my house. She had to go back home and change, in order to meet you guys."

"Wow. I don't think I knew that."

"No. Mom was down in the bakery, and it was a slow day. So she didn't need my help. And Yolanda came in through the back. I'm not sure Mom even saw her come or go."

"That explains it. You are the only one who knew."

"I know. And I feel so guilty. I could have just let her stay. I could have put my book aside, shared my kittens, and Yolanda would still be with us."

"Do you think so?" Claire asked, her head tilted.

"Yeah. I'm sure of it," Lauren said, seeing the doubt on her face. "You're not?"

"I guess I just feel like if it's God's will, it will happen. But if it's not God's time, then it's not going to happen. So, if He was ready for Yolanda to go home, it didn't matter what you said or did, she was going home when He wanted her to."

Lauren had never thought about it that way before. Maybe that was part of the reason why she had decided that she needed to talk to her friends.

"It's interesting. I'm not changing the subject. But I had my mind set on what was going on in my marriage. My husband was the bad guy entirely. And yet, when I came here, and talked to you guys, and talked to Skyler, I realized that my view was not the only view. I think that's part of the reason I decided that I wanted to talk to you guys about that day. I thought that maybe you'd have another view." She looked at Claire. "I like that idea. I'll have to think about it to see whether or not I really truly believe it, but I know that God is in control of everything. He makes the sun to shine on the just and the unjust, and the rain to fall on the same. If He can control the sun and the rain, He can control the affairs of man. And I suppose that while He does move for the prayers of man, and He changes things according to how we pray, even sometimes when we pray, God just says no."

"He's told me no more often than I wish, but sometimes when I look back, I think, man, I was dumb for wanting that. The older I get, the more I have a tendency to pray, 'God, You do what You know is best, and help me to handle it.'" Grace laughed, and the other two joined in.

"That's probably a really good prayer. Because...my way just leads to messes, like me leaving my husband."

"God might have allowed that. After all, your husband is out here, and now he might be selling his business and you might be opening your mom's bakery, and none of that would have happened if you hadn't left. I'm not saying God wanted you to, but I'm saying that God works everything out for our good and His glory, even our stupidity and dumb mistakes."

"Thanks. I actually feel better about that now." And she realized, she also felt better about Yolanda. Claire and Grace were probably both right. That if it had been God's will for Yolanda to live, she wouldn't have died that day. No matter what Lauren had done.

"I know you feel selfish because you wanted the kittens to yourself, and you wanted to be able to read your book and all of that." Claire put her hand on Lauren's arm. "I feel guilty because I didn't insist that we wear life vests. None of us were wearing them. But I wasn't a better swimmer than Yolanda was. So why did she drown and I didn't? Why did I bob up with a life vest right beside me? And the boat on the other side. I got the life vest on, grabbed hold of the boat, and everything was just fine. I don't know why."

"Same. I could have insisted that we wear life vests. I could have insisted that we turn around sooner. I could have done a lot of different things, and I felt guilty about that for years. But the fact of the matter is, it doesn't really matter what I would have insisted on. If the Lord willed it, it didn't matter. Because God is stronger than anything I can do. And He's not dependent on me doing something in order to have something else happen. He can control the wind and the waves. Obviously."

"And that was a rogue wave. I don't know if we ever talked about it, but it came up out of nowhere. There was a storm coming in, but that wave was..."

"It was different than any of the other ones. And I'm not saying it was sent exactly by God, but He could have controlled it. We know He could have."

Lauren looked at her two friends. She didn't realize that they had been carrying around guilt all these years too. She wished she would have talked to them a long time ago. They all felt bad. They all blamed themselves. And there really wasn't any reason for them to do that. Even if they were wrong, there was nothing they could do to bring Yolanda back. The past was the past, and it was done. Finished. And it couldn't be changed. She just had to move forward, hopefully learning from her mistakes and trying not to make the same ones again.

She could do the same thing in her marriage. She did feel bad for leaving her husband. But maybe she could learn from that mistake, like her friends had suggested, and not make the same mistake again.

"Not to change the subject, but I kind of wish that I would have thought about buying the inn. I didn't even realize it was for sale."

"I'm pretty sure it was sold, but I don't know who bought it. But maybe they'll sell it again."

"The last time I looked, I wasn't sure what I was looking at could be saved."

"I happen to be married to someone who's pretty good with his hands," Grace said.

"I suppose you and Trevor together could have done something with it. But...it's going to take a lot of money."

"You'd only have to get one or two rooms ready, and you could rent those out while you worked on fixing the rest of it."

"I think you'd need to get the outside done so that people who look at it don't think the whole thing is going to fall down around their heads."

"If I remember correctly, there were almost solid walls of windows, and it was kind of up on a hill so it had a gorgeous view of the lake. And the sunset over the lake. And...wasn't there a restaurant or something attached to it? And...it was just very romantic." Lauren tried to remember. She hadn't been there much before it closed down back when she was a kid.

"We didn't have a lot of money, and I don't remember ever going there."

"We didn't have a whole lot either, but it was one of the only places in town where you could get food, and when my mom had a day off, she never felt like cooking."

"One of the drawbacks of owning a bakery. You don't like to cook for yourself. Like a cleaning business owner, right?" Grace laughed.

The others joined in, and they talked about light things, easy things, things that friends talked about. And then, Lauren remembered about the dog.

"Have either of you heard of anyone missing their dog?"

"I don't think so," Claire said, glancing at Grace.

"No one mentioned it at Bible study today. I would have thought that that would be a good place for someone to ask, if they were looking."

"I have a stray dog coming around the back of the bakery, and it seems like she's pregnant. I'm not an expert on dogs or anything, but she seems close."

"You always liked animals. And babies especially," Grace said, and Lauren thought about the kittens.

It was true. She was always taking in one stray or another and enjoying it.

Of course, when she had a roomful of puppies, she was taking on the responsibility for trying to find them homes. Maybe she wouldn't be able to do that. Maybe it would be best if the dog never did learn to trust her. But they'd gotten dog food today at the grocery store, and she was going to give it her best effort.

"All right. I suppose I better get up and get back to my husband and children." Claire stood, and the others followed suit.

"Is your ex-husband really not wanting them at all?" Grace asked as they moved to walk back down the trail.

"Nope. He had them for two weeks, and he basically called begging me to take them back. He said he'd see them at Christmas. And I was fine with that. In fact, it made my summer."

"There are so many fun things to do with kids beside the lake," Lauren said.

"And we are pretty much trying to do them all. I'm remodeling the kitchen and painting the outside of the house. It's definitely a full summer."

"I think it's important to stay busy. And keeping kids occupied is a good way to keep them out of trouble." Lauren believed that to be true. It was what her mom always said. That's why she had worked in the bakery after school. But she never really thought of it as a job. Because her mom gave her lots of leeway to be creative, and she was allowed to experiment with different things. That was how she got so good at making Nutella banana bread and the cheese bread which was her signature.

Her mom had definitely encouraged her creativity while gently guiding her away from things that were not good for her.

They stopped at the gate and embraced.

"Thanks for meeting. We'll see you next week, same time?" Lauren said, realizing they hadn't really settled that.

"If not before then, that sounds good to me," Grace said, and Claire agreed.

"I can pretty much make any time, as long as I know ahead of time, so I can make sure that the kids are good."

Lauren felt light and happy as she walked down the sidewalk. Maybe things were going to work out after all.

Twenty

"Are you ready to go?" Lauren asked as she finished wrapping the loaf of Nutella bread she was going to deliver to Skyler before she and Cannon took a walk along the beach.

"I am," he said, looking up from his phone, then clicking a couple more times before he turned it off and shoved it in his pocket.

"I can carry that," he said.

He'd finished putting the security system in the day before, and she'd allowed him to sleep on the couch that night. But that wasn't where he wanted to be.

"How do you feel about calling Josiah and seeing if he'll let us take a look at the house? I was thinking that we should grab it while it's available, because it's so close."

"Really?" she asked, sounding surprised.

"Unless you wanted a place further out? But then there would be a longer commute for you to come here."

"I guess we could rent out the apartment upstairs."

"Yeah. Or we can keep it for out-of-towners who want to visit, or we could even add to the bakery, have a sitting room upstairs where people can take their baked goods and read or something."

"That would be perfect if Matteo was still opening a bookstore."

"He's not. He's got a buyer for his books already, and he's shopping around for exercise equipment. He actually asked me if I would give him a hand putting something together tomorrow."

"That's nice," she said, seeming surprised.

Maybe she didn't realize that in the time he had spent outside putting the security system in, he and Matteo had developed a bit of a friendship.

He'd even asked Matteo for some tips on beginning a workout routine, and Matteo had offered to give him some one-on-one training.

He wasn't going to tell Lauren about that, unless she specifically asked. It wasn't that he was hiding it, it was just...he was a little embarrassed to admit that he even needed to. He wasn't sure why. It just...was a subject he was kind of touchy about for some reason.

He pushed the door open, held it while she walked through, and allowed it to shut. He'd already engaged the alarm and felt satisfied and at peace that he was doing a good job of taking care of things.

Probably because he owned a security company, but it was extra important to him.

"It's a beautiful day," she said as they walked along the sidewalk toward Skyler and Homer's house.

There were a bunch of kids playing in the yard, and Skyler and Homer sat on the front porch.

It looked so cozy and quaint, like a fun, all-American family and something he might have expected to see in the sixties.

That was one of the draws of Raspberry Ridge. It was just one of those small towns that didn't seem to age.

He had mixed feelings about the rumors that they were going to have more tourists this year. On the one hand, it would be good for Lauren's bakeshop, on the other, he wanted Raspberry Ridge to stay the way it was. Because it was pretty much perfect.

"It is. I can't wait to see the beach you keep talking about."

"I can't believe we've been together for more than a decade and you've never been on the beach in my hometown."

"We'll remedy that today."

"But first, banana bread for the neighbors." She held it up. And then waved to Skyler. "Hey there!" she called.

"Lauren!" Skyler jumped up and hurried off the porch and to the sidewalk. "You look so happy. What a beautiful day for a walk."

"Yeah. My husband's never seen the beach, so I'm taking him to show it off a bit. But I wanted to deliver this to you. I appreciated your advice. It was spot on."

Skyler smiled and slid a glance at Cannon. Cannon had the uneasy feeling that somehow her advice had pertained to him.

"Hey there," Homer said, coming over and holding his hand out.

Cannon shook it. "It's good to meet you. I've heard a good bit about you. I'm Cannon."

"Yeah. I've heard a good bit about you as well. I know that my wife has invited you guys to the Bible study that we typically have here on the porch, but I understand that Lauren thinks it might interfere with her business opening. Still, you're invited and welcome any time."

"I'd really love to come. I've heard lots of good things about it. My neighbor, Matteo, has been there a couple of times, and as much as I'd love to attend, I'm afraid we probably can't unless it gets moved to the shop."

"I'm fine with moving it there, but I don't want Lauren to have to provide food every time, because that's not fair."

"I know she wouldn't mind, but it probably would be bad for the bottom line."

"Yeah. That's my thought."

"Why don't we do it on the porch in the summer and then move it to the shop in the winter? She still wouldn't be required to provide food every time, but it would give us a sheltered place and maybe give her a little bit of extra business, if people bought coffee and whatnot from her then."

"We could have a special discount, just for the Bible study people in the morning," Lauren added.

"That sounds like a great idea," Skyler said.

Homer put his arm around her, and she looked up into his eyes, and they smiled the smile of people who knew each other well and liked each other anyway.

Their kids played in the background, squealing and yelling and sounding like they were having a great time, not paying any attention to the adults at all.

"All right. We'll let you guys get back to your family time. But I just wanted to say a little thank you." To his surprise, Lauren took hold of his hand as they walked away.

He loved the way her fingers felt in his and tried to recall the last time they'd held hands.

To his shame, he couldn't remember.

"I've missed this," he said, holding up their linked hands.

"Me too," she said, smiling over at him.

They went a little farther until she said, "Instead of going into the healing garden, you take this path right here. It does get a little steep, and it's probably best to do it single file."

"All right. Do you want me to go first?"

"I can. It's not very far."

She was right. It was a short path, maybe fifty yards or so, although there was a switchback, and it was definitely steep.

Once they hit the bottom, there was a little bit of a grade until they reached the pebble beach, but the waves were louder, and the view of the lake was beautiful. The deep blue sky and the slightly more mysterious blue of the lake complemented each other, accented by the white of the breaking waves.

"Wow. There really is no sand."

"No. I told you. Now, it does get sandy up that way, but this is probably my favorite beach anywhere."

"The pebbles are all smooth, worn away by the waves, and it would be a good beach to go barefoot on."

"Why not?" she asked, kicking off her flip-flops.

He had been wearing socks and shoes, and it took a little bit until he got them off. He'd rather walk with his shoes on, but it seemed more in the spirit of things for him to go along with the carefree nature of his wife.

"I don't think I've ever seen you walk anywhere barefoot," she said, watching in disbelief as he took his shoes off.

He was glad he had, just so he could see that look. Like she didn't think he was going to, and he'd just proved her wrong.

"I'll get used to it," he said, winking at her.

She laughed outright at that.

He set his shoes beside her flip-flops and deliberately took her hand again, looking into her eyes as he did so.

She smiled up at him, and he felt content. Like...maybe things were going to work out.

He had ordered her something, and it was supposed to come that afternoon. Maybe it would be there by the time they got back. He had been checking on it on his phone before they left.

He thought that it would say to her that he was thinking of her and cared about her. At least, he was hoping it would.

"So George is unable to get the money to buy my company."

"That's too bad. But I wasn't sure I wanted you to sell it anyway."

Did she really mean it? Half the time, he thought maybe she was just saying it, but Lauren wasn't the kind of person who just said things, so she must have been sincere.

"Why not?" he finally settled on. The beach was beautiful, the breeze felt good on his face, but even better was the feeling that he and Lauren were right with each other again. He couldn't believe how much he'd neglected her trying to build his business.

"It just represents a lot of years of work for you."

"And I'll get that back in money. It might be enough that it won't matter whether or not your bakery is successful. We might be able to do it just for fun. You know?"

"So basically we retire?" she asked, wrinkling up her nose.

"Sure. Why not?"

"I don't know. We're kind of young."

"We could do something. I don't know, have a little business on the side along with the bakery. Something online maybe, or I could put in security systems up here, just not on the biggest scale. I don't think I have any interest in trying to build another company." It had been a lot of work. He didn't want to get sucked into it again.

"I'm happy to hear that, although I am proud of you for building something out of nothing. I do want you to know that."

"You made a lot of sacrifices in order for me to do that." Maybe it was just getting away from the business finally, but he felt completely detached from it, and he really wouldn't care if someone made an offer tomorrow. He didn't even think he'd feel bad when he signed the papers.

"I want to talk about kids." That was something that was important to her, and he'd been giving it a lot of thought.

"Okay," she said carefully. As though she knew that was a bit of a minefield for both of them.

"I know you talked about the miscarriages and how much they hurt. And we never really talked any more about that. Do you...want to look into medical reasons why we might not be able to have a full-term child? Or would you rather look into adoption? Or something else?"

"Well. I don't know. I...guess I hadn't given it any more thought."

"Well, we're not getting any younger. And that was the other thing I was thinking. I sell the business, and we'll have time to be parents. Now, we'll have to be careful with our money, of course, but depending on how much I get for it, we could probably do whatever you wanted to. I don't think cost would be a factor."

"I heard that adoption can be an expensive option."

"It can be. That's what I'm saying. We'll have the funds."

"Unless of course we foster kids and then adopt them."

"You wouldn't want a baby?" he asked carefully. That had seemed to be her dream.

"I guess I do, but...I want children more. You know? Like we saw the kids running around in Skyler and Homer's yard. It was just so much fun. It felt like an old-fashioned family where everyone is just together, and...I really want that."

He had to admit he'd felt the pull too when they had been there. "I can understand that. It just feels old-fashioned and...safe in some way."

"Yeah. When a mom and dad create a haven for their children to grow up in. I mean, I know it's not going to be all roses and bluebells, but I do think it would be nice."

"I understand what you're saying. That's kind of why we're here, other than to bring glory to God, to fill the earth and subdue it. That is our command."

"Yeah." She spoke softly and a little bit dreamy. He wished he could give her a healthy baby. He really did.

"I think part of the reason that I had such a hard time being sympathetic about the miscarriages was because I really wanted to be able to give you a healthy baby, and I felt like it was some kind of failure on my part that we couldn't do it. It was something I couldn't control. And I don't like dealing with things that I can't fix on my own, you know?"

"I do know. It's like the security system. You want to get in there and do something. Not stand around and talk about it."

"Right. I mean, I love talking about ideas, but when there's a problem, I don't want to just talk—especially a problem like that, where I know that I don't have the ability to stop the miscarriage or to stop your tears or your pain."

"Thanks for saying that. It does make it better. It helps me to be a little bit more understanding of why you weren't around, because I really had a hard time wondering why you weren't more upset and why you weren't more concerned about me."

"Yeah I just did the easy thing. I made sure you were okay, and then I went to work. The harder thing was to stay and do what wasn't comfortable, which was to hold you, even while I felt helpless and frustrated."

"It helps that I know that that's how you felt. I don't like the idea that you don't feel good about it."

"I don't think anyone feels good about that. You were in pain and crying, I was frustrated and helpless. We just dealt with it in different ways, I guess. Or it brought out different feelings in us."

"I see what you're saying."

They had been walking for a while, and she suggested that they turn around.

He agreed, and they walked slowly back down the beach.

"I'm not sure where this new direction that we're going is going to take us. I'm not talking about us doing the same old thing."

"No. I knew. You're talking about leaving the company, selling it, moving here, doing the bakery, possibly children, and who knows what all else."

"Exactly. It's exciting but a little bit scary at the same time."

"Yeah. I get mostly excited feelings, but every once in a while, I have this anxiety that comes over me and I wish I had my mom. It's almost like a wave of grief, but it's combined with fear. I feel like I'm alone."

"You're not alone. You're with me."

"I know. And your sister and her husband are part of our family, though they're pretty far away."

"I think we have a good network of friends here in Raspberry Ridge. There are a few other people I keep hearing about but I haven't met yet, and with the bakery, I bet we'll be seeing everyone."

"I bet you're right. I guess Mom would smile if she could see this."

"I think that's probably what you need to keep in your mind. The fact that your mom would be happy if she could see what was going on. I mean, it's sad that she's not really here, but her memory is." He quit talking, trying to find the words that would comfort her. He shook his head. "I'm sorry I'm not very good at this."

"Not very good at what?" she asked, tilting her head as she looked at him, their joined hands swinging between them.

"Finding the right words to comfort you."

"I just appreciate you trying. And I appreciate even more you being here beside me. I feel kind of bad that I threw such a big fit."

"You don't need to say that again. I think you pulled us back from a very bad spot and got us going in a direction that I'm excited about. Moving to Raspberry Ridge, looking into starting a family, buying a house, doing your mom's bakery, and all the new neighbors that we're meeting. It's pretty awesome. I'm glad you did what you did."

"Thanks. That's very reassuring." She sighed. "I know you're right. But...you weren't a bad husband. What I did was a little over the top."

"I thought I just said we weren't going to say that anymore." He laughed, tugging at her hand and pulling her closer to him. He pulled his hand out of hers and put his arm around her, holding her close. "I love you. I'm glad you did it. I don't know how much more time I would have wasted wrapped up in my own bubble on the treadmill of trying to make more money and become bigger and better and chasing all those things that don't really matter."

She stopped, and they turned and faced each other.

"This could have been very different. If you hadn't been so humble and willing to look at yourself and believe that there was a problem. I mean, we could have been separated or even divorced."

"No. I wasn't going to let that happen."

"I know. I'm just saying, it's because of you that that didn't happen. And I am deeply, deeply grateful."

He could see the sincerity in her eyes, and he hoped that she saw the same in his.

She must have seen something she liked, because she took a step closer and wrapped her arms around him. It had been a while since he'd felt that, and it felt perfect and right, the way a yard full of children and parents sitting on the front porch on a summer afternoon felt perfect and right.

"I love you," she said to him, and the words settled deep in his soul.

"I love you too," he said, and she lifted her face, and he did the most natural thing which was to lower his head and touch his lips to hers, the feeling familiar yet brand-new at the same time. And absolutely perfect, like it always had been.

He had to admit, kissing his wife on the beach was very romantic.

He wasn't sure how long they stood there, but an exceptionally strong gust of wind made them lose their balance, and they broke apart, laughing.

"I guess that means we're supposed to keep moving," he said, reaching for his wife, putting his arm back around her.

"I guess so."

He pulled his phone out of his pocket, checking because he thought he'd got a notification, and he saw that what he had ordered had been delivered.

"I have a surprise for you back at the bakery."

"You do?" she asked, furrowing her brows like she couldn't possibly imagine what it was.

"Yeah. I'm kind of excited about it. I shouldn't spoil the surprise, and I'm not going to tell you what it is. Just that it's there, and I think you're going to like it."

"All right," she said, laughing, as they went back to where they'd left his shoes and her flip-flops, and they put them on before they started up the trail, him feeling like everything was right in the world.

Twenty-One

"What in the world could you have gotten me?" Lauren wondered aloud as they got closer to the bakery and she saw there was a big box sitting outside.

Big. Huge.

"What in the world?" she asked, thinking at first maybe it was some kind of newfangled mixer, but it was long and wide, not deep.

"I want you to open it," he said. "And there's a second package, a small one, behind the first."

"I can see. It says right here what it is," she said, turning her head so she could read the words that were sideways since the box sat on its end.

"A kiddie pool?" she asked, furrowing her brows and looking back at him.

"Yeah," he said, letting the word just hang there.

"What in the world are you getting me a kiddie pool for?" she asked, even as she bent down to look at the smaller box. That one was in a packing box, and he quickly got his pocketknife out so he could cut the packing tape, and she could open it.

Inside was something in a piece of plastic that was shrink-wrapped.

"This is a...dog bed!" she said, jumping up, comprehension dawning in her eyes. "You got a kiddie pool to put in the shed along with the dog bed so that the stray dog can have her babies in there!"

He nodded, grinning.

"Oh my goodness! This is awesome!" She reached for him, kissing him hard on the lips, before she said, "Can we put it up right now?"

"Sure," he said. He'd measured the shed before he ordered the kiddie pool to make sure that it would fit. He'd already moved some things around while she had been busy doing some baking, when she thought he was outside working on the security system. Everything was ready, all they had to do was take it out of the package and set it up.

Plus, they needed to tame the dog down, but from what Lauren said, she was coming every morning and every evening for a little bit of food. Lauren said she hadn't tried to pet her, but that was mostly because he had asked her not to unless he was with her, and he hadn't been there.

He appreciated her considering his feelings on that matter.

The kiddie pool box was not heavy, but it was awkward, and they basically slid it back between their building and Matteo's shop.

Then, Lauren went back to grab the dog bed while he opened the box and got the kiddie pool out, setting it in the shed. It fit perfectly, like he thought it would, and he had it sitting where it needed to be when she came back with the dog bed.

"I think this will probably take a little bit of time to fluff out."

"Yeah. It's supposed to be a lot bigger than that, so it should fluff out a good bit."

She smiled at him as he took his pocketknife and cut across the top.

She set it in the kiddie pool, and then they went about gathering up the garbage and placing it neatly beside the building where they could grab it and deal with it later.

When they came back, the dog bed was indeed fluffing out.

"I think I should unfold it," Lauren said as she climbed into the kiddie pool and started messing with the dog bed.

From his calculations, the dog bed wasn't going to fill up the kiddie pool. He wasn't sure if they would need to worry about puppies getting caught on the other side of the bed, or whether it would be okay. He really didn't have a whole lot of experience in doing this, but apparently Matteo had heard his buddies talk about doing this in the military.

Regardless, it had made his wife squeal and act almost like her old self, and it had been worth it. Even if he had to deal with the dog and however many puppies.

"I really wanted to get something that we could put in the house, but...if we're going to try to renew the old permits and get a license to open the business, we really can't do that."

"No. No animals in the house at all. Maybe that's part of the reason why I have always loved animals so much. They were a definite no in the house when I was growing up, although we had a couple cats outside."

"If we go look at Josiah's house, we can keep animals there. Since we wouldn't be living on top of the bakery."

"That's another point in favor of getting a house," she said. "You don't have to talk me into it."

A small whine interrupted their conversation.

Cannon had been so interested in what they were talking about, he hadn't even thought about where the dog might be. But as he stopped and turned carefully, they saw her standing just three feet outside the doorway, her tail wagging, her belly drooping almost to the ground.

"Oh my goodness. She wants to come see her new bed," Lauren said, although Cannon wasn't quite sure that was exactly what was going on.

"I wanted to name her Lacey, by the way. Is that okay with you?"

He wanted to shrug his shoulders and say something along the lines of "I don't give a flip what you name the dog," but he thought that maybe she really did care about his opinion.

"Lacey sounds like a good name. She looks like a Lacey."

As he'd suspected, his interest made his wife smile, and it was a smile and look that lingered on his face before she turned back to the dog, crouching down.

"Lacey. Look what we did for you," she spoke softly, in a coaxing voice.

"We got some treats with the dog food, didn't we?" he suddenly remembered.

"Oh. We did. I actually haven't given her any of those yet."

"Okay. Brace yourself. I'm going to walk slowly over to the corner. Do you keep the treats with the dog food?"

He knew that the dog food bag was in the far corner of the shed. They had put it there after carefully checking to make sure that there were no leaks and it wouldn't get wet.

"Yes. They're unopened and sitting beside the bag."

He walked slowly over and decided that it might be best for him to open the bag there to keep the rustling and any extra noises as far away from Lacey as possible.

Lacey seemed like maybe a little bit of a fancy name for such a scruffy dog, but perhaps once she got cleaned up, it wouldn't be so bad.

He wasn't sure how many to get, so he grabbed four. Two for Lauren, and two for him.

"Here you go," he said, putting two treats in her hands. Moving slowly and carefully so as not to scare the dog.

But he really needn't have worried. Either she was extra hungry or extra happy to see them.

She came right over, and as Lauren held a treat on the palm of her hand, with her fingers flat out, Lacey came over, sniffed, and took it up delicately, as though someone had taught her not to snatch treats from human hands. Or to be careful not to bite human fingers when she was getting a treat.

"I think she might let me pet her," Lauren said, looking up at him with questioning eyes.

She didn't say the words aloud, but he almost felt like she was looking to him to make sure it was okay.

"All right," he said. If she got bit, he was ready to tackle the dog, and they would deal with whatever they had to deal with.

The dog did have a collar, so it had been someone's pet at one time from the looks of it. And if they could get close enough and manage to get her to the vet, maybe they could figure out whether or not she was microchipped, since there was no license. Sometimes collars had little tags with their names on them, but he didn't see anything like that on hers either.

"She ate them both!" Lauren said as Lacey took the last one.

"I'm holding two more."

"Why don't you try to give them to her?"

"If I'm going to give her treats, she's going to have to do something to earn them."

"She came the whole way over here and allowed us to feed her. That certainly deserves a treat."

"But these are two new treats. She has to do something new."

"All right. Like what?" she asked, looking up at him and lifting her brows.

"I suppose we could try to get her to get into the kiddie pool, but I think that might be a little bit much."

"Yeah."

Instead of that, he turned to Lacey and said, "Sit."

To his surprise, and to Lauren's astonishment, Lacey's rear end went down on the ground.

"Oh my goodness. She's trained!"

"She sure is. Good girl," he said, holding the treat out, only this time instead of holding it on his palm flat out the way Lauren had done, he gave it to her with his fingers wrapped around it.

She took it just as politely as she had the other two.

"Someone's definitely worked with her. Which makes me wonder, did someone drop her off because she was pregnant? Did someone just abandon her? Or did she somehow get separated from her owner?"

"I think I'm going to try to take a picture and see if I can post it online in a few different places, to see if anyone recognizes her."

"That's a great idea. Let me see if we can get her to stand up again."

He moved back just a bit, although there wasn't much room with the kiddie pool behind them. But Lacey got up and took a step toward him.

"That's a perfect position. Just hold on a second," Lauren said as she held her phone out and snapped the picture.

She did a few more things, which he assumed was her posting the picture online with a comment asking if anyone recognized her.

"Do you think it would be okay for us to close the shed and keep her inside?" Lauren looked at him questioningly. She was practically in the shed, and it wouldn't be hard to close the door behind her.

"I don't know." He supposed that if they put food and water in there, she would be fine. "Is there a way we can just enclose her in the yard? And leave the shed door open? That way, she might find the kiddie pool on her own, and if she has the puppies, at least she'll be around."

"There is a fence and a gate in the back, but she's been getting in and out through a hole that she, or a different dog or animal, dug under the fence. I can't keep her in."

"Well then, we have two choices. We can make her stay in the shed, or we can just allow her to choose us."

He felt like the second option was a better one, but he was guessing that Lauren would go for the first. After all, the dog really didn't know what was best for itself, and that's why it needed owners.

But for Cannon, it meant more when she chose them. It was kind of the way he was allowing Lauren to choose. He could have come and demanded that she go back to him, and they could have fought and ended up breaking up completely, because instead of wooing her, he'd commanded her.

Now, he knew what the Bible said about men being in charge of the household and women being submissive and obedient. And he would have had every right to stand in front of his wife and say, "You have to listen to me because the Bible says so." But sometimes, at least in his newfound wisdom, that wasn't the best way. Sometimes the best way was to woo things to oneself.

After all, that was the way God worked. He had all the authority in the world to stand in front of any human and say, "I demand that you worship me," and the Bible clearly said that that was the way it would go someday. But for now, God had given them free choice, and He stood, wooing them. Wooing them with beautiful sunsets, and fresh lake breezes, with sweet smiles from people he loved, and the bonds of neighbors and friends. With summer storms and winter snows and a sky brimming with stars at night. That's how God drew them to Himself. And that's how he wanted to draw his wife back. With love and warmth and all the ways he could show her that he cherished her.

"I think we ought to just leave the shed door open and let Lacey decide if this is where she wants to have them." Lauren stood from where she had knelt before the dog, scratching her ears. "After all, I don't want her to have the puppies in the shed on the floor as she scratches to get out, unhappy because she's penned up."

"I think that's a really good idea. Let's try to make it so that she wants to stay here."

"I think that's the best idea," Lauren said, and he wasn't quite sure what she was thinking as their eyes met and she smiled at him. A sweet, loving smile, the kind that he hadn't seen for years and years, but now they came easily to her face.

All it took was a little attention and some love from him, and her entire countenance toward him had changed.

Why hadn't he done this earlier? Why hadn't he paid attention to her sooner?

He couldn't answer those questions, other than maybe he was just so consumed with trying to be successful, enjoying himself even in his quest to be successful, because he saw it as a challenge, he saw it as fun, it was something he had enjoyed. But in his pursuit of his own happiness, he'd left the most important person in the world to him behind. And that was all on him. He vowed that it wouldn't happen again.

Twenty-Two

"I really love this huge picture window right by the dining room table. The view is amazing."

"When we remodeled the house back when I was a kid, Mom insisted on lots and lots of windows. The Michigan winters get dark and cold, and she wanted to let in as much light as possible. She never even put curtains on that window."

Josiah spoke quietly from behind where Lauren and Cannon stood. He had immediately allowed them to take a look at the house, saying that he would love to have friends and neighbors buy it rather than anyone else.

His parents had already moved to New Mexico and were counting on him to sell it. He had put up a little homemade "for sale" sign before engaging a realtor, just because he was hoping that someone from town would see it and know someone who knew someone, or something along those lines. Apparently, his gamble had paid off, Lauren thought to herself, because she didn't know about Cannon, but she was in love with it.

"I love how your mother has decorated things. She and I have a lot of the same tastes." Maybe she would rip out all the old carpets and put down hardwood floors if they had the money to do that, but otherwise, she loved the clean white walls, the pops of color in the décor, and all of the beautiful, large, and open windows.

"My mom grew a lot of plants too. She took most of them with her, but there's definitely enough light to do that if you want to."

"I love plants. And there's room in the back for a garden too."

"Yeah. Once upon a time, Mom had that, but she hasn't had that for years and years."

"You look like you're really enjoying this." Cannon finally said something.

"What are you thinking?" she shot back, rather than answering his unspoken question. Yes, she was loving the house, but she didn't want to get it if it wasn't something that he wanted too.

He had been so sweet and kind and considerate of her over the last few weeks since he'd come to Raspberry Ridge. She wanted to return all of the goodwill that he had bestowed upon her.

She knew that he would say that her leaving him had been the best thing that could have happened, but she didn't think it was right. Not even a little bit. In fact, she knew it had been wrong. She had no biblical leg to stand on, and even though God had used her sin and worked it out for their good, it might not have turned out that way. It might have ended in divorce and a broken family, which is not what God wanted. And her disobedience could have had terrible consequences. Thankfully, her husband had covered her sin with love. Just like it said in the Bible. Love covers a multitude of sins.

Instead of coming in, as he rightfully could have, and demanding that she go back, and not apologizing for anything, because neglecting her, not spending time with her, was no sin in the Bible. But her husband had chosen to be humble, had chosen to hear the cry of her heart, and had chosen to respond to it in a loving and Christian way. She figured she would probably adore him until the end of time, just because of that.

"I say if it makes you happy, it makes me happy too. I would be happy living in the shed behind the apartment building, if that's where you wanted to live."

She laughed. "Lacey would have to move over."

Lacey hadn't had the puppies yet, and she looked big enough to pop any day, but she had discovered the bed in the kiddie pool that they'd made for her in the shed, and most mornings when Lauren went out, that's where she found the dog, slowly getting up from where she'd spent the night in the kiddie pool.

"This is perfect. I love everything about it. I love the location, I love the fact that there are four bedrooms that we could fill with children eventually, and I love the tons of windows and even everything down to the nice big kitchen. It's my dream home." She lifted her shoulders. It even had a nice big porch with a swing on it, where they could sit and swing and watch the cars go by as their children played in the front yard with the big shade tree. Perfect for a tire swing, and there was even room for a swing set, unless they wanted to put that in the back and forget about the garden.

"All right then. Looks like we'll be making you an offer. I felt your asking price was fair."

"Mom and Dad wanted to price it below market value for a quick sale. We didn't have an appraisal, so you can always do that just to make sure the pricing is in line, but we did some research and felt like we were priced about ten percent below what the actual value would be."

"I agree. I actually did some research online before we came, and the price you quoted us is more than fair." Cannon spoke, and then he looked at Lauren. "I think we'll want to talk about it a little bit, just to make sure that we're both really on the same page, but I'm pretty sure you can expect an offer from us."

"That's great. I'm not sure exactly how that process works, but we can figure it out. It can't be that hard."

"People buy and sell houses every day. And somehow they figure it out. I think we can too."

Cannon held his hand out, and Josiah shook it as they grinned at each other.

Lauren smiled as she watched her husband. He could definitely figure it out. There wasn't too much that he couldn't figure out. She felt confident that everything would be fine. But she just wanted to take this moment to admire him a little, his confidence and his competence. And the knowledge that she was secure trusting in him. That he wouldn't lead them wrong. That he might go in a bad direction, but that he would listen to her if she said to him, "I don't think this is a good idea." Maybe he would eventually still continue to go in the direction that he felt was best, but the idea that he would stop and listen to her, consider her, and make sure that she knew that she was loved and cherished by him, made all the difference to her in the world.

She wasn't sure what made the difference to him. Maybe it was just having her there. Knowing that she wanted him. That she wanted to be loved and cherished by him so much that she would disrupt a comfortable, financially secure life in order to have his attention and his love.

She hoped that was what he saw. It was what she wanted him to see. She didn't want him to think that she was faithless and fickle and wanting to run from man to man, just to satisfy her ego or her psyche. And Cannon didn't seem to think that at all. He looked at her and saw the very best. What more could a woman ask from her husband?

And what more could she do for him in return than the same? To look at him and see the very best? And to allow love to cover a multitude of sins.

As they walked out of the house, holding hands, which they had done everywhere they'd gone since that day on the beach, he looked down at her. "Is this truly what you want?"

"Yes. It's a perfect house. In a perfect place, in the town I grew up in, and the town I would love to raise my children in, but more importantly to me, I want to know what you want. Because the most important thing to me is that you're happy."

She knew that was true now. It might not have been true a few months ago. Because when it came right down to it, she'd left because she wasn't happy. Not because he wasn't. He was fine. He was just perfect. But what had prompted her to leave their home, and leave her husband, had been selfishness and unhappiness on her part.

Instead of trying to take the situation and change it, and if she couldn't change it, to pray about it until she was content, and to look and see that her husband was fine.

"I believe that. You know, I know this is crazy, but this was one of the hardest things in my life. To think that my wife might leave me, to think that I wouldn't have this." He held up their joined hands. "That you might not live in the same house as me and might decide that you wanted a different man."

"I never even thought about that," she said honestly.

"I know. But those thoughts went through my head. Fear, and an absolute determination that I needed to change, because you were more important to me than anything. But without going through that hard time, that agony of not knowing whether or not my wife was going to stay or leave, I wouldn't have grown in ways that I can't even imagine— that I couldn't even imagine that I needed to.

"I guess what I'm trying to say, and I'm not doing a very good job of it, is I'm grateful for the trial. I'm grateful that it turned out well, even more so, but I'm grateful because I feel like I have a better relationship with you now than I did before. And that is worth it all."

"You know, I was thinking about that when we were standing in the house. It's because you covered my sin with love. That's why it worked out well. And I will be grateful for that for eternity." Because he'd saved their marriage. It was all him.

He shook his head though, unwilling to take the credit. "God was in it. God knew all along, and He works everything for our good and His glory."

She had to nod. She couldn't disagree.

"And He's opened the door here. I love the house too. But I didn't want to say how much until I heard from you, because I was afraid that you would be okay with getting it, just because I thought it was perfect."

"No. I hope I'm always honest with you. I mean, I'll do things that you want just because you want them, but I hope if you ask my opinion, I'll tell you my honest one."

"I don't want anything else."

They had stopped outside the gate and were standing, talking to each other face-to-face, their hands joined between them.

"Another really great thing about that house is the proximity to the bakery. Less than a block away. It will be so easy to go back and forth. I can picture kids running between the house and the bakery and back again."

"Will we have children?" she asked, wondering if maybe that just wasn't something that God had planned for her. It might not be something He was going to give her, and she had to be okay with it. She thought she was, truly, okay with it.

"We talked about adoption. And going through the foster system. I'm good with that if you are."

"I am too." She didn't know what to do about the miscarriages. She supposed that they could do something to prevent them. Or they could just let it go and see what God did. She supposed she would be open to that, although the miscarriages tore at her heart, and she wouldn't mind if she never had another.

"Well, after we close on the house, I think that should be our next step. Seeing what we need to do to figure out how to adopt a whole bunch of kids. And give them the very best home we possibly can."

"I agree. That sounds perfect."

"But for right now, let's go check on Lacey. She just didn't seem quite right when we left."

"I agree." Lacey had been pacing around and going in and out of the shed, although she was ignoring the kiddie pool and the bed that she normally slept on. Lauren had been afraid that perhaps Lacey saw the bed as something that she slept on and not something that she would have her puppies on.

The dog had really tamed down in the last week, and she was pretty sure that wherever she had puppies, she would allow them to move the puppies into the kiddie pool. That was if she had them in their yard. Although for the last several days, she hadn't left the yard.

"If she has those puppies in our yard, I'm going to fix that hole under the fence and make sure the gate works and latches, and we're going to consider Lacey ours unless someone comes to claim her."

"Yeah. I guess the first time we take her to the vet, we'll need to see if they can check for a microchip, but beyond that, I'm in total agreement." She didn't really want to. She loved Lacey, and the idea of giving her up now made her stomach clench, but if Lacey were her dog and had somehow gotten separated from her family, she would appreciate someone doing everything possible they could to reunite the dog with the previous owner. So she couldn't do any less herself.

They walked across the street, still holding hands, and she walked first between the two buildings. She had a feeling that grew stronger as they got closer to the shed in the backyard by the shady groves of peach trees.

But she didn't say anything. Not until they got to the backyard, and she looked around, and then she walked cautiously to the shed.

Somehow, it was no surprise at all that when they put their heads in, Lacey lay in the pool, with two wet and wiggly puppies beside her, and she seemed to be pushing on a third.

"My goodness. She chose us. She chose us!" Lauren looked with shining eyes at Cannon, whose own eyes were suspiciously wet.

"She did indeed. She did indeed." But he wasn't looking at the dog when he said that. He was looking at her. And she got the feeling that he was thinking about her and that she had chosen him. It was true. She had. Forever.

"Hey! So sorry I'm late. But that's the way it is when you take kids to school," Claire said as she and Josiah walked in the door to the Monday morning Bible study.

They were having it in the bakery for the first time. They'd just opened the Saturday before, and since school had just started, and the mornings were getting colder, they thought it was a good time to move the Bible study indoors.

Lauren had been more than happy to host it. Eventually, they might remodel and redecorate the upstairs of the apartment to accommodate the study upstairs. She thought that was a great idea, and she was pretty sure that it was on Cannon's list of things he wanted to do.

First though, he was going to help Matteo put a security system in. Matteo, who was at a table, deep in conversation with her husband, had asked him a few weeks prior if he could price one out.

Of course, Cannon had been able to pull a few strings and still had contacts where he could get one at cost, and the labor of putting it in would be free. They wanted their neighbor and good friend to be successful in his business, and they were willing to do anything they could to help him.

She now sold energy drinks, as well as a variety of special waters, just to cater to his clientele.

They also looked into foster care, and they were meeting a family of four small children on Wednesday.

Lauren could hardly wait, and she hoped that the puppies, which were going to be eight weeks old, would not go to their new homes until after the kids got to meet them.

She and Cannon had tried as hard as they could to find an owner for Lacey, but no one had stepped forward. Now their only difficult decision was whether or not they were going to keep Lacey and one of the puppies or just Lacey.

Still, they had homes lined up for three of the five, and if they were going to keep one, they needed to make a decision soon.

Lauren took the tray of Nutella banana bread over to the tables that they had joined together so that everyone would have a seat at the Bible study. Cannon had already provided water, and since it was the first day that Bible study was going to be held in her bakery, she had said that she would provide the refreshments.

They had agreed that it would not be her responsibility all the time, but...she was going to have a hard time not doing it. Especially since Cannon's business had sold for millions more than they had expected, and as long as they were wise with their investments and prudent in their spending, they were set for life, as were their children and grandchildren. She couldn't imagine having that kind of wealth, and they'd spent a good bit of time studying investments over the last eight weeks. Almost as much time as they'd spent studying the material that the foster care people had given them.

Life was looking up. It was unbelievable to her that just a few months ago, she thought she was at her lowest point ever.

Maybe it was true, that old adage, "It's darkest just before dawn." Maybe it's never time to give up. Maybe making the decision to stay in her marriage, to work at it, to do what God wanted, rather than what she wanted, was the best decision ever.

She put a hand on her stomach as she walked back to the counter to grab the second tray of sticky buns.

It could end up being a false alarm or could end up in another miscarriage, but she also had reason to hope that perhaps this time, God was going to bless them, not just with a family of adopted children but also with a child of their own.

Whatever God gave them was good, and she would take it with thanksgiving. It was something she was working on but was still not perfect at, but it was her goal. Because God was good, all the time. Even when it seemed like He wasn't.

Thanks so much for reading! If you'd like to head back to Raspberry Ridge and enjoy lakeside breezes, the nostalgic scents of summer and home and more sweet, second chance romance, you can get Through the Dark Night HERE.

Sneak Peek of Through the Dark Night

Raspberry Ridge 2 miles.

Shannon adjusted her grip on the steering wheel, her hands sweating. Just two miles until she was...home? It felt like she was coming home. But she didn't want to. She left for a reason, and she hadn't looked back, taking her two children and leaving with her husband, heading out of the town she grew up in.

Too many painful memories.

Now, with her marriage blown to bits and her children scattered, leading new lives of their own, she felt like this was the only place for her to go.

Sure, she could have stayed in Detroit, but...who wanted to live in Detroit?

She had friends there, but they were city friends, friends from the suburbs. People she waved to, saw when she was out walking, knew by first name, and that was pretty much it.

They weren't the kind of friends who knew the details of her life, both the good and the bad, the ugly.

Most of the time, that wasn't what she really wanted. But she missed the soul-deep knowledge that small towns had. Sure, there was gossip, and nothing was off-limits, but there was a caring there, a concern, a "you're one of our own, and we will take care of you" kind of attitude that was completely lacking in the generic Detroit suburb.

She swallowed hard and took a breath. Why was she nervous? Why was she scared?

Maybe it wasn't nervousness or fear but more a knowledge that the memories were here, and she'd never faced them. Everyone said time healed, and Shannon believed that to be true. Surely allowing time to put a buffer between her and the sharpness of the pain was a coping mechanism that would someday be acceptable in the eyes of the world.

She wouldn't change the fact that she left.

She might have changed some of the decisions that she made when she was younger, but she pushed that thought aside as well. Her life was what it was, and there wasn't anything she could do to change it now. The decisions had been made, consequences had been lived through, and there was no turning back.

However, sometimes a person got to a fork in the road and they had to make a decision about how they were going to move forward.

She already made that decision too. She decided that she was going to sell the house in the suburbs and move to Raspberry Ridge.

And now, here she was, almost back in her hometown for the first time since she left almost two decades ago, and she felt like turning around and running.

She had no idea where she would run to.

As her white SUV crested the last hill, the expanse and magnificence of Lake Michigan came into view. The sun glittered on the water, and Shannon's breath caught in her throat. Grateful that the road was deserted, she pulled to the side of the road and came to a stop, her hands resting on the wheel, her eyes on the immense and beloved lake in front of her.

This was her last view as she left town all those years ago, her heart cracked and broken, and she wasn't sure she would ever be able to function without pain again.

The pain had faded, although she had come to understand that it would never truly go away. One could not lose one's daughter—a child that had come from one's own body, one that she had nurtured and cared for for the first fourteen years of her life—and not expect there to be a permanent mark on her soul.

She pulled both lips in between her teeth as she looked at the rippling water, the sunlight glistening, always moving, shimmering and shining, then dark, cloudy, and dreamlike.

She couldn't figure out whether it felt good to be home, or maybe she just felt relief. Relief that she had a soft place to land after all this time.

Of course, the landing might not be as soft as what she hoped. She shoved that thought aside. She would face that when she had to, but first, she had to get into town.

Taking one last long look at the shimmering lake in front of her, she took another deep breath, as though to fortify herself for the last, and hardest, leg of her journey, before she pulled back out on the highway.

No cars had passed. At least that hadn't changed. Raspberry Ridge was a beautiful little gem that not very many people knew about. If tourists knew, they would flock here, although they'd have to find a different place to stay, since the old inn had long ago shut down, although Shannon could remember pieces of it from her childhood.

Still, that was more than forty years ago, and so much had changed. So much. She tried to push those thoughts aside. Change wasn't necessarily bad, but it was easier to swallow in small doses.

She was face-to-face with the fact that because she hadn't been there for almost twenty years and had decided to come back to live without visiting first, she was going to have a lot of big doses of change.

Her car moved slowly down the highway, as though she wanted to put off the inevitable for as long as she could, but soon the first houses of Raspberry Ridge came into view. The same, yet different. Older, more paint chips, more weather-beaten. They'd been through almost twenty Michigan winters, which was no small thing, especially along the lake.

Winter had always been fun to her, lots of snow, lots of things to do —skiing and sledding and building snow forts and castles and playing with her children in it, even ice-skating at times. Winter had been her favorite time of the year, and she'd always been a little disappointed when the snow had melted and spring had sprung.

Not that she didn't love Michigan springs and summers as well. Fall was maybe her least favorite time, but it held the promise of another winter coming.

Now that she was older, the cold got to her more, the wind felt chillier. Her coats and winter clothing didn't keep the chill out like they used to. Maybe she would hate winter. Maybe this was a big mistake. Maybe she should have gone to Florida.

She kept puttering along. There was the church on the hill. The old one that had closed before she had left and before the new one closer to the lake had opened. That's where the grave was. The one she hadn't visited in almost twenty years. What kind of mother was she to have not visited her daughter's grave in all that time?

She felt guilt clogging up her throat, but she pushed it down. Forcefully. After all, she had taken the absolute very best care of her daughter while she had been alive. She had been the very best mother that she could possibly be. Who cared whether she took care of the grave after her death?

Suddenly she had an urgent need to see it. But she was already past the place where she needed to pull off, and she kept going.

There, at the end of the dead-end street, she could see the healing garden that had taken the place of the old gazebo that had sat there all through her childhood. It had started to decay and fall, and the town had demolished it before her children had been old enough to hang out there like she and her friends had.

They had had so much fun sitting in the gazebo, talking, making plans, using it as a meeting point for a trip to the pebble beach.

So many memories, and yet the gazebo was long gone.

She turned her head and saw Fran's store.

Almost without thinking, her hands turned the wheel, and she pulled in along the street, parking right in front of the store that didn't seem to have changed at all since the day Shannon had left. She had stopped here and bought a soda and a bag of chips for both of her children. They had been a good bit younger than Yolanda at eight and ten, and she hadn't wanted to have a whole lot of questions, she hadn't wanted to have to talk to them. So, she convinced her husband to stop, and she'd run in and gotten them what amounted to bribes to stay quiet for the trip to Detroit.

James hadn't wanted to stop, not when they were just getting started, but she insisted.

She couldn't even think about James, so she put those memories aside to think about later too. It seemed like that was what she did with everything her whole life, set it aside until she was able to handle it. When would she be able? Here she was, fifty years old, and still didn't feel like she was adult enough to face all the pain and heartbreak in her past.

But she definitely couldn't think about that now. Not if she was going to go into Fran's, which apparently she was since she had parked the car right in front of the store.

Part of her wanted to go in, to see what had changed, and part of her wanted to run in the other direction.

Deliberately putting her hand on the latch and yanking hard, she opened her door and stepped out, adjusting her purse over her shoulder and squinting in the bright sunlight. She adjusted her shades and closed the door, walking with determined steps to Holloway's General Store.

The bell jangled over her head as she opened the door and stepped in. It wasn't hard to recognize Fran, who was adjusting some candy on a shelf right in front of the checkout counter. Her hair was white, and there were definitely added pounds, which gave her figure a more matronly look than what Shannon remembered, but Fran wasn't the only one who had a more matronly look.

She didn't look like she was in her twenties anymore either. Although, she had been thirty-four when they left. With three children, she'd been slender, maybe not teenage slender, but she definitely didn't have the matronly figure that many mothers of three did. Not then anyway. She'd gained weight since the divorce, although she lost it before it had been finalized. Sleepless nights, wishing she could have done something to keep her family together, wondering what she could have done to prevent her husband's infidelity, and constantly trying to tell herself that she had done the best she could, and there was no point in looking back.

Fran straightened and turned around. She blinked and then tilted her head as Shannon removed her sunglasses.

Shannon didn't really expect Fran to remember her. It had been almost twenty years.

"Shannon McKay, well, I'll be... I guess it's not McKay anymore, is it?"

"Actually, it is McKay." That had been the first thing she'd done after her divorce was final. If James didn't want her anymore, she wasn't going to keep his name. Her kids had been a little upset with her. They hadn't wanted to have a name that was different than hers, but they hadn't wanted to ditch their father's name either, and she had not encouraged that. She had gently suggested that the name that they were born with was the name that they identified with. She encouraged them to not do anything rash. After all, James had been a good father. If by good, one ignored the fact that he had cheated on his wife and broken up his family, committing adultery and leaving a wake of pain and devastation behind him.

Fran's face fell, and her brows lowered. "Oh? I hadn't heard."

The gossip hadn't reached Raspberry Ridge? Shannon supposed that made sense. After all, she didn't have any ties left in Raspberry Ridge. Both of her parents had passed on in the last five years, and her siblings had long since fled. She stayed in touch with them but not on a daily basis. It was more like she picked up the phone for Thanksgiving or Christmas or maybe texted them on their birthday. And they did the same for her.

She nodded.

"I'm sorry to hear that," Fran said, sounding truly sorry as she bustled forward, her arms outstretched. And if her walk was a little bit less steady than it used to be, if she seemed a little bit more frail, Shannon ignored it as she allowed the older woman to wrap her arms around her and envelop her in a cinnamon-scented hug.

It felt like home.

Without thought, she felt herself hugging back, tightly, the kind of hug a person gave someone they knew and loved and missed.

"I'm sorry I mentioned it," Fran said, stepping back and looking up at Shannon, almost as though she was hungry for a good look at her.

"It was amicable." She didn't feel like she was lying when she said that. Her husband and she were still talking. She could call him up today, he would answer her call, and they would have a civil conversation. However, she knew there was a part of her that resented what he did, that was hurt in a way words couldn't explain over the fact that he had walked out on their almost thirty-year marriage. That he had obviously not even tried to make things right between them. He hadn't suggested counseling, hadn't even told her that there was anything wrong. She just intercepted a text his girlfriend had sent, and he'd come clean about everything and moved out that same day.

"Well, that's good to hear. So many times, there's so much fighting and bickering that the lawyers get everything and a person has to be careful about what they say." Fran waved her hand. "But Raspberry Ridge seems to be the place for second chances lately. You wouldn't believe the people who have come back and found love here. It's...been good for my old heart to watch."

"That's not going to happen to me. But I am back to stay."

"You are? Are you looking for a place to rent?" Fran asked, and Shannon figured that if she was, Fran would certainly know of the places that were available.

But she wasn't.

She thought about hedging or dodging the question, but there was no point. Raspberry Ridge was a small town, and everyone was going to know sooner or later. It might as well be now.

"No. I bought the old inn."

Fran froze, her eyes opening wide in shock. "That was you?"

Shannon nodded. She had set up an LLC and bought it under that, not necessarily to keep the townspeople from knowing that it was her, although it had that effect as well. But it was more for tax purposes. Her accountant had suggested that was the way she should go.

"Well, I'll be," Fran said, a hand going to her heart. "I can't believe it." She huffed out a breath. "Mind you, I'm happy about it, because having that old inn opened up, fixed up, generating revenue, and bringing people in could be nothing but good for this town. But... I would never have guessed that it would have been you."

Shannon nodded. She didn't want to go into the whole divorce and her needing to have something to do, a purpose in life. She felt worthless, with her kids gone and her husband gone and her rattling around that big old house in the 'burbs of Detroit by herself. The one that held all the memories of her raising her children and their laughter ringing in the walls, the late nights she'd spent staying up with them holding them while they were feverish or coughing, the times James had come home with good news from work, a raise, a vacation, and just the regular old family time around the table in the evening as they ate supper together.

All of it was there, crumbling in on her, crushing her, making it so that she could barely breathe. She needed a new start. But she didn't want to do something completely new, like move to Florida. She needed a new start in an old spot, one that was familiar and welcoming and one where she knew she could heal.

Raspberry Ridge was the only place that could happen. And what better thing to do than to fix up the old inn? It would be new, yet it was old at the same time. It was in her memory, but the memories weren't so personal that she couldn't handle the pain. After all, if she tried to move back into the house that they'd owned when Yolanda had died, she wouldn't have been able to handle it.

Thankfully, that house was not along the main street, and she hadn't seen it coming in. If she didn't want to, she wouldn't have to see it at all. Because she would have to make a concerted effort to pull into the driveway and drive back to the house. And then it would be a little awkward as she sat there while the owners wondered what in the world the crazy woman was doing staring at their house.

Yeah, that wasn't going to happen.

"So are you just here scoping it out? How long are you staying?"

"I'm here for good."

She didn't elaborate, and Fran looked a little confused. Shannon knew that wasn't the way people usually operated.

"Oh my goodness. And James... James isn't with you?"

Shannon shook her head. She knew that Fran was just digging for information, but she didn't feel ready to share that, even though she wasn't trying to hide anything. She wasn't the one who had done anything wrong.

"It's been a long drive, and I'm here for some coffee. Do you have some?" she asked, although she could smell it when she walked in.

Fran nodded and pointed at the coffee machine that sat at the end of the checkout counter.

Shannon walked up and got herself a cup as Fran chattered about the changes that had been happening in Raspberry Ridge since she had left. She also talked about some of the things that hadn't changed a bit.

Shannon paid for her coffee, and then she escaped out of the store without giving out any more personal information. People were going to find out eventually. It was a small town, and that's what happened in small towns, but it didn't have to be today. She had a little bit more time to herself before she had to share more of her life with the world, or with Raspberry Ridge, which was the world when one lived in a small town.

She took two steps toward her vehicle before the sight of the healing garden caught her eye.

On a whim, she turned and walked the fifty yards to the entrance. She had heard via an article in the local paper that Raspberry Ridge had put in a healing garden. The article had been more about Dominic and Vera Miller, the award-winning duo who had built the garden, than it had been about Raspberry Ridge, but the setting had been what had caught Shannon's eye.

And now, as she read the plaque that was visible from the gate, she remembered that the article had said that Dominic and Vera had lost a child.

To those who are waiting in heaven for us.
This is a place where we can sit and remember, wish you were still with us,
be happy for your good fortune, and look forward to the day when we are
reunited.

She didn't remember reading about the plaque in the paper and wondered if maybe it had been added later.

The words were perfect though. Because Yolanda waited in heaven, and since the day of her death, Shannon had been looking for a way to heal and had been looking forward to them meeting again.

This was definitely a place she wanted to get back to. But as she saw the sun lowering in the sky, she knew she had to move on. She didn't know what she was going to find when she got to the inn, and she needed to face that for sure.

With one last look at the plaque and then the healing garden in general, she turned and walked back to her car.

In some ways, this had been harder than what she thought, and in some ways, she felt stronger just for what she'd been able to accomplish, coming to town, walking into Fran's and chatting, and seeing that the town was just as welcoming as it always had been. And then, knowing there was someone else who shared her grief and sorrow and who had gotten through it, using that grief to do something to be a blessing to other people.

Maybe that was what Shannon was doing with the inn, using her grief and the heartache that she had endured to be a blessing to others. The thought made her smile.

A Gift from Jessie

View this code through your smart phone camera to be taken to a page where you can download a FREE ebook when you sign up to get updates from Jessie Gussman! Find out why people say, "Jessie's is the only newsletter I open and read" and "You make my day brighter. Love, love, love reading your newsletters. I don't know where you find time to write books. You are so busy living life. A true blessing." and "I know from now on that I can't be drinking my morning coffee while reading your newsletter – I laughed so hard I sprayed it out all over the table!"

Claim your free book from Jessie!